Praise for the authors of
THE SUMMER HOUSE

SUSAN MALLERY

"Susan Mallery is warmth and wit personified.
Always a fabulous read."
—*New York Times* bestselling author
Christina Dodd

"Ms. Mallery's unique writing style shines via vivid
characters, layered disharmony and plenty of spice."
—*Romantic Times*

"If you haven't read Susan Mallery, you must!"
—*New York Times* bestselling author
Suzanne Forster

TERESA SOUTHWICK

"Ms. Southwick's fetching characters and emotional
impact keep reader interest high."
—*Romantic Times*

"Teresa Southwick dishes up effective romantic
tension and good character interplay."
—*Romantic Times*

Dear Reader,

While taking a breather from decorating and gift-wrapping, check out this month's exciting treats from Silhouette Special Edition. *The Summer House* (#1510) contains two fabulous stories in one neat package. "Marrying Mandy" by veteran author Susan Mallery features the reunion of two sweethearts who fall in love all over again. Joining Susan is fellow romance writer Teresa Southwick whose story "Courting Cassandra" shows how an old crush blossoms into full-blown love.

In Joan Elliott Pickart's *Tall, Dark and Irresistible* (#1507), a hero comes to terms with his heritage and meets a special woman who opens his heart to the possibilities. Award-winning author Anne McAllister gets us in the holiday spirit with *The Cowboy's Christmas Miracle* (#1508) in which a lone-wolf cowboy finds out he's a dad to an adorable little boy, then realizes the woman who'd always been his "best buddy" now makes his heart race at top speed! And count on Christine Rimmer for another page-turner in *Scrooge and the Single Girl* (#1509). This heart-thumping romance features an anti-Santa hero and an independent heroine, both resigned to singlehood and stranded in a tiny little mountain cabin where they'll have a holiday they'll never forget!

Judy Duarte returns to the line-up with *Family Practice* (#1511), a darling tale of a handsome doctor who picks up the pieces after a bitter divorce and during a much-needed vacation falls in love with a hardworking heroine and her two kids. In Elane Osborn's *A Season To Believe* (#1512), a woman survives a car crash but wakes up with amnesia. When a handsome private detective takes her plight to heart, she finds more than one reason to be thankful.

As you can see, we have an abundance of rich and emotionally complex love stories to share with you. I wish you happiness, fun and a little romance this holiday season!

Karen Taylor Richman
Senior Editor

Please address questions and book requests to:
Silhouette Reader Service
U.S.: 3010 Walden Ave., P.O. Box 1325, Buffalo, NY 14269
Canadian: P.O. Box 609, Fort Erie, Ont. L2A 5X3

Susan Mallery
Teresa Southwick

THE SUMMER HOUSE

Silhouette

SPECIAL EDITION™

Published by Silhouette Books

America's Publisher of Contemporary Romance

SILHOUETTE BOOKS

ISBN 0-373-24510-6

THE SUMMER HOUSE

Copyright © 2002 by Harlequin Books S.A.

The publisher acknowledges the copyright holders of the individual works

MARRYING MANDY
Copyright © 2002 by Susan Macias Redmond

COURTING CASSANDRA
Copyright © 2002 by Teresa Ann Southwick

Visit Silhouette at www.eHarlequin.com

Printed in U.S.A.

CONTENTS

SUSAN MALLERY

is the *USA TODAY* bestselling author of nearly fifty books for Harlequin and Silhouette, as well as mainstream and historical romances. Frequently appearing on bestseller lists, she makes her home in the Pacific Northwest with her handsome prince of a husband and her two adorable-but-not-bright cats.

TERESA SOUTHWICK

lives in California with her husband of twenty-five years and has two handsome sons. Reading has been her passion since she was a girl, and she couldn't be more delighted that her dream of writing full-time has come true. She has written over fifteen books for Silhouette, and has also written historical romance novels under the same name.

MARRYING MANDY

Susan Mallery

Dear Reader,

My writing career began in January 1989 when I walked into my first writing class. It was given at a local adult education center and the teacher was the only published author I had ever met. It was darned exciting, I have to tell you. We went around the room and each said what we'd written to date. I'll admit I was proud of my fifty pages. Then a woman sitting behind me announced she'd written an eight-hundred-page book. Wow!

The class was eight weeks long and by week six, I knew I'd found what I wanted to do for the rest of my life. I also made some friends in that class, one of whom joined me in a critique group where we read each other's work and offered advice. That friendship, begun all those years ago, continues today.

Teresa Southwick is the woman who wrote that eight-hundred-page historical romance. Those of you who have read her books know that she usually writes for Silhouette Romance. Now she is also writing for Silhouette Special Edition.

Terry and I came up with the idea of writing a book together—one about two girlfriends sharing a summer vacation at a fabulous beach house. They have great plans for a "girls only" break, but romance is in the air and two handsome men have other plans for our friends.

Please enjoy your chance to get away from winter for a little California sun in our very special 2-in-1 book.

All the best,

Susan Mallery

Chapter One

"If the sex was amazing, why wouldn't you want to see him again?"

Mandy Carter held the phone at arm's length and stared at the receiver. No way she'd heard what she thought she'd heard. It wasn't possible.

"You can't know anything about our sex life," she said as she tucked the receiver back into place between her ear and the crook of her neck. "And if you do, *I* don't want to know about it."

On the other end of the phone, Joanne Benson laughed softly. "I know a lot more than you think I do."

"That scares me. I'm sorry, Jo, but talking to my ex-mother-in-law about my former sexual relationship with her son is just too weird for me."

There was another chuckle. "Your generation thinks it's so hip and together, but the reality is you're all a bunch of prudes. I came of age during the sixties and I have to tell you, that was a real sexual revolution.''

''I can only imagine,'' Mandy muttered, not really wanting to.

''So…was it amazing?''

Mandy threw down the granny square she was trying to crochet as part of a baby blanket for yet another pregnant co-worker. ''You're making me crazy.''

''Then answer the question. I know what Rick said. I'm curious about your take on things.''

Mandy was suddenly curious, as well. What exactly *had* Rick said about their sex life? Or was this all a bluff on Jo's part? After all, mother and son might be very close, but Mandy doubted they'd actually talked about his sexual escapades.

''I'm changing the subject,'' she said firmly.

''Fine. Change away. Or let me change it for you. If you don't want to talk about sex, why don't you at least get in touch with him? It's been a long time. You two used to be friends. Wouldn't you like that back?''

Be friends with her ex-husband? ''I don't know,'' Mandy said honestly. ''I've done fine without him this long.''

Mandy and Rick had met and married nine years ago. They'd divorced less than a year later. In all the time since, she'd never once spoken with him. Oh, she knew about his life. Being close friends with his mother meant that she was kept abreast of all his successes. She knew that he'd completed his Ph.D. program in record time, that he'd parlayed his genius in the world of laser physics into an incredibly lucrative career. That six years and multiple money making patents later, he'd quit to take on a different kind of challenge. He was currently working for some exclusive high-tech think tank in Santa Barbara.

She also knew there had been several close calls but no second marriage.

"You're going to practically be neighbors," Jo said lightly. "Have lunch with him. What would it hurt?"

Mandy was less concerned about pain than how strange it would be. But she thought a lot of Jo and didn't want to disappoint her friend. "You're not matchmaking, are you?"

"Of course not. That is *so* not my style. However, I will admit that I think it's interesting neither of you has remarried. I can't help wondering if there's some unfinished business between you and Rick. If so, a lunch might help you both to move on. If nothing else, I would like two people I care about very much to at least be speaking to each other."

"Fair enough," Mandy said, only a little concerned about meeting with her ex. But what was there to worry about? She and Rick hadn't seen each other in eight years. She never thought about the man, except when Jo mentioned him.

Besides, Jo had a valid point. She had remained friends with her son's ex, while maintaining a close, loving relationship with him. Most divorcing couples argued over ownership of pets or custody of children, but Mandy and Rick had been forced to deal with sharing Jo. After years of not having a mother, Mandy hadn't been willing to end a relationship with her charming, caring mother-in-law, not even with a pending divorce on the horizon. Rick was close to his mother and had been unwilling to break ties with her, as well. In the end, they'd agreed they would both have relationships with her, even if they didn't have one with each other.

For the past eight years, Jo had been a rock for Mandy. A confidante, someone to have fun with. A real and loving friend. Which made Mandy unable to refuse the request, even if it did sound strange.

"I'm staying in Carpinteria for a month," Mandy said. "That's only about twenty minutes from Santa Barbara. I promise to get in touch with him while I'm there. If he's willing to have lunch, then we'll break bread together. Does that make you happy?"

"Ecstatic. I'm all aquiver."

Electrons were tricky, Rick Benson reminded himself as he scanned the printout of the latest test and saw the experiment hadn't produced the results they had anticipated. This was a third no-go, which meant he would not be recommending funding. He initialed the top of the report, scribbled comments in the margin and made a mental note to prepare for the outrage that would follow his decision.

He knew this project was one of the board's favorites, but if they didn't want to know his opinion, they shouldn't have bothered to ask him.

The phone next to him buzzed. He hit the intercom button.

"Benson."

"Hey, Rick. Two things. John Samuel called again. He wants to know if you have a recommendation yet."

Rick shoved the report into his out basket. "Tell him I have one, but he's not going to like it."

Clara, his secretary, winced. "Maybe I'll wait until

I know he's in a meeting, then leave it on his voice mail.''

Rick grinned. ''Chicken.''

''You bet. I hate being yelled at by members of the board. On the one hand they think you're brilliant, on the other hand, they hate it when you stand up to them. And I'm always the one stuck leaving messages.''

''Then use e-mail.''

''I'll think about it. Oh, I almost forgot. You have a phone call. Someone named Mandy Carter. You want me to put her through?''

Mandy? His first thought was that his caller was a different person with the same name. His second was concern that something had happened to his mother.

''I'll take the call,'' he said, and reached for the receiver.

''Benson,'' he said sounding more curt than he'd meant to.

''Hi, Rick. It's, ah, Mandy…um, Carter. Your ex-wife.''

She sounded nervous, not worried, which told him that she probably *wasn't* calling to tell him something was wrong. He relaxed back in his chair.

''I know who you are,'' he said, surprised to find himself pleased to hear her voice. It had been a hell of a long time.

''Okay. I wasn't sure.'' She cleared her throat. ''So, how are you?''

''Good. Busy. Yourself?''

''The same. Well, probably not as busy as you. I'm a teacher and I have a month more off before classes start again.''

"That's right. Mom mentioned you'd gone into that. Special ed, wasn't it?"

"Uh huh. I work with elementary-school-age kids. It's rewarding but grueling. I'm glad for the break. A friend offered to let me stay in her family summer home in Carpinteria for the month. She's joining me in a couple of weeks."

"Sounds like fun."

He knew that Mandy had lived in Los Angeles after their divorce. She'd finished her college education, then had gone on to get a master's.

Which didn't explain why she was calling after all these years.

"So here's the thing," she said as if she could read his mind. "I was wondering if you'd like to have lunch."

Rick was now more surprised by her invitation than by her phone call.

"Why?" he asked before he could stop himself.

Mandy laughed. The sparkling sound did odd things to his concentration.

"It would make your mom happy. She made me promise to call. She thinks we have unfinished business together, which I think is crazy, but you know how she is when she gets an idea in her head."

"She becomes the immovable object."

"Exactly. So I figured it was easier to just say yes. Hence the invitation. Are you game?"

Up for lunch with Mandy? He could honestly say he hadn't given her more than a moment's thought in the past few years. But the idea of seeing her again, of talking with her, was strangely appealing.

He pushed a button on his Palm Pilot. "When?"

"Rick, I'm on vacation. My schedule consists of

things like reading and watching old movies. You're the one with meetings and projects. What's good for you?''

He scrolled through his electronic calendar. He didn't have anything free until a week from Tuesday. Damn.

"How about tomorrow?" he asked, knowing Clara was going to kill him for messing with his schedule.

"Sounds good to me."

"There's a place on the pier in Santa Barbara. The last restaurant on the left—a fish place. We can get a table by the water. Say noon?"

"I'll be there."

"I look forward to it."

They said their goodbyes and hung up. Talk about a blast from the past. He wondered if Mandy would look the same or different. He remembered a tall, slender redhead with big green eyes and a smile bright enough to light the world. They'd literally run into each other on campus one afternoon. He'd taken one look at her and had fallen hard.

He'd proposed within four months, they'd been married within a year and separated less than eight months later. The speed-of-light set of events had left him shaken. He'd managed to dust himself off and get on with his life. Obviously she'd done the same.

Getting together after all this time would be fun, he told himself as he e-mailed the schedule change to Clara. They'd talk about old times, then go their separate ways, probably not to see each other for another eight years.

Mandy was nervous. She couldn't believe it, but the roller-coaster sensation in her stomach didn't lie. She was actually nervous about seeing Rick again.

Rather than give in to growing panic, she turned her attention to the beautiful view before her. The pier stretched out into the ocean. It was early August and a perfect Southern California kind of day with blue skies and warm temperatures. The tang of salt water perfumed the air. Dozens of tourists walked the length of the pier, peeking into store windows and reading restaurant menus. They looked happy and carefree. She would bet none of them were having lunch with an ex.

She stepped around a toddler with a teetering ice-cream cone and past a family with three kids, each wearing a bathing suit and holding a balloon animal. Compared to the out-of-town crowd, she was over-dressed in a simple light-green sundress and sandals with two-inch heels, but it was hard to know the appropriate kind of clothing for lunch with an ex-husband. She'd left her long hair loose. Looking at her no one would ever guess that she'd spent nearly two hours trying on every outfit she'd brought with her for her vacation, nor would they ever know that her casual cascade of curls was the result of an entire morning spent in electric curlers. Some things were better left a mystery.

She spotted the restaurant up ahead. Her stomach zipped around a forty-five-degree angle, going about a hundred miles an hour. The sensation was far from pleasant.

This was a really stupid idea, she told herself as she walked along the pier. Really stupid. The next time she spoke with Jo, she was going to tell her so. And what had she, Mandy, been thinking by calling

Rick on her second day of vacation? Why hadn't she put it off until the very end? Why had she—

There were tables set up in front of the restaurant, small spots for patrons to wait or gather. Brightly colored umbrellas provided shade. As she approached, a tall, dark-haired man stood and moved toward her. A tall, dark-haired, really *good-looking* man with broad shoulders and the kind of hunky, filled-out body that deserved its own billboard campaign. A man without thick glasses or a faint frown, or a book anywhere to be seen. A man who sent her stomach into a five-G dive and made her normally sensible heart start to pitter-patter. A man who was smiling at her as if he knew her. As if he'd been married to her.

She stumbled to a stop. "Rick?"

He grinned. Oh, yeah, a real macho, tempting grin. Nothing so simple as a smile. While Mandy watched him approach those last few steps she had the feeling that the new and improved version of Rick Benson was going to be big-time trouble.

"Mandy," he said, when he paused in front of her, continuing to grin that mind-stealing grin.

There was an awkward half second when she didn't know if she was supposed to shake hands or start a hug or do nothing physical. She couldn't recall reading any etiquette column about this particular dilemma.

But Rick solved the problem by bending slightly— had he always been so many inches taller than her?— and drawing her against him. The semi-A-frame hug should have been completely platonic, but she had an instant sexual flashback, which was crazy because their sex life had been borderline okay but nothing that exciting, whatever he might have told his mother.

She had a brief impression of heat, strength and confidence that made her toes tingle, then he lightly kissed her cheek and stepped back.

"It's been a long time," he said, his voice low and sexy. Had it always been like that? She couldn't remember, and then he took her hands in his, so she couldn't think. "You look good."

"You, too," she managed, forcing the words past slightly numb lips.

Surprises had a way of sucking the life out of her brain. Not a really good thing to have happen when one was dealing with a man who had an IQ about double the national average.

His hold on her fingers was light, yet she didn't feel she could pull away. Something to think about later, she told herself, along with the fact that she should have felt weird about him touching her hands after all this time and she didn't.

He studied her, still grinning, as if he liked what he saw. "You've kept your hair long. It's nice."

"Thanks. I thought about cutting it, but I'm too chicken. For work I have to keep it back in a braid, but the rest of the time I wear it down."

Argh! Could she have sounded more inane? What on earth was wrong with her?

He released her hands. "I made a reservation," he said. "We can go in now and get a table, or sit out here and talk for a while."

She considered her options. Standing this close to him was doing bad things to her knees. She kept feeling as if they were going to give way at any moment. So sitting down and staying seated seemed like a really good idea.

"Let's go in now," she said.

"Great. This way."

He indicated the direction with one hand and rested his other on the small of her back. She felt every inch of skin touching her through the dress as if she were being burned by a brand.

Hmm, not exactly a brand, she thought. The pressure was far too nice for that. But something hot. Something that made her want to move closer and rub like a lonely house cat.

Obviously, seeing Rick after all these years had made quite an impression on her. She'd expected to feel awkward, but she hadn't expected to be blown away. Honestly, she hadn't expected a lot of things.

Chapter Two

They were led to a table by an open window that offered a perfect view of the ocean. Mandy lowered herself onto the chair and was grateful for the soft breeze that drifted across her face. Maybe fresh air would help keep her senses straight.

Rick sat across from her. Although she couldn't help thinking that her ability to speak in anything close to full sentences would be greatly increased if he was across the room...or maybe even in another restaurant.

The hostess handed them menus. Mandy took hers without opening it and laid it across her place setting. There were several boats out on the water and children playing along the shore. Lots and lots of activity to capture her interest. But instead of gazing out at the view, or the people, she found her attention drawn to the man sitting across from her.

His eyes were the same blue as the water below, she thought. A deep, dark blue. She was unused to seeing his irises so clearly—normally he wore thick glasses, which blurred the color. Well, not when they'd been in bed. While they'd made love, she'd been able to clearly see his eyes, which made looking at them now a distinctly sexual activity. Like she needed to sweat her attraction to him even more!

"It's the glasses, right?" he said cheerfully. "You're not used to seeing me without them."

"Exactly."

"I had the laser surgery a few years back. Now I have perfect vision."

She winced. "I don't think I could stand the thought of someone pointing a laser at my eyes. I'd be forced to run screaming from the room."

"You never wore glasses so you don't know what a pain they can be. I was forever having to push them up. When I started scuba diving, I wanted to be able to see the fish and whatever else was floating around down there. My corrective mask helped, but not enough. Once they perfected the procedure, I went ahead and had it done."

Mandy stared at him. "Scuba diving?" she repeated. As in being in the water, getting wet and swimming? Rick? The man who considered turning on his computer close enough to a sport to call it exercise?

"Wow," was all she managed before the waitress appeared at their table.

The woman was petite and blond, with a bright, sassy smile and a gaze that lingered on Rick. "Would you like something to drink?" she asked, focusing all her attention on him.

Rick barely glanced at her. "Mandy? What would you like?"

"Just a diet soda," she said.

"I'll have iced tea," he told the waitress.

The young woman nodded and left. Mandy had the impression that Rick had noticed her interest in him and had not been impressed. Talk about a change. Eight years ago if a woman other than Mandy even spoke to him, he generally started blushing and dropping things.

He leaned toward her, his elbows on the table. "You're very much the same, only better," he said lightly.

"Thanks. I could say the same about you."

He chuckled. "I'm not a nerd anymore?"

She eyed his muscular arms, visible in his short-sleeved shirt, and the breadth of his chest. From there she admired the square set of his jaw, the killer blue eyes and mouth that curved at the corners.

"No hint of a nerd at all."

"I sent in for one of those study-at-home courses," he confessed in a low, teasing voice. "From the James Bond school of male behavior. I have a small pistol tucked into my sock."

"I'll be on my best behavior."

The waitress returned with their drinks. She still seemed to notice only Rick.

"Are you ready to order?" she asked him. "We have several specials."

Rick shook his head. "Why don't you give us a little time? We have a lot of…catching up to do."

The waitress finally glanced at Mandy. Her mouth twisted. "Lucky you," she muttered as she left.

Mandy laughed. "That James Bond course really paid off. She's smitten."

Rick dismissed the comment with a wave. "Okay, I didn't take a course, but I have changed. I guess I grew up. After MIT, I got a job that put me out in the real world for the first time. I traveled a lot, met different people, experienced things. It all had an impact. I like to think it was an improvement."

She couldn't help wondering how many women had been involved with his "experiences." Probably a lot. Not that it was her business. Although she did wonder where he'd learned to send out such sexual vibrations. Even sitting down she could feel her knees knocking slightly.

"You were terrific before," she said easily. "Although I'll admit the package is a little more polished now."

He nodded his thanks. "And you?"

"I like to think I've matured. I managed to turn thirty this year without sobbing myself to sleep."

"Thirty looks amazing on you," he said. Then before she could respond, he raised his iced tea. "To growing up, and to old friends."

She touched her glass to his, even as she wondered if they could be considered old friends. They had been married for nearly eight months, then they'd parted under unfortunate circumstances. There had been a lot of pain, but time had healed, as it was supposed to.

"Tell me about your life," he said. "I hear a few things from my mom, but not the details. How long have you been teaching?"

"For six years now." She thought of her kids and smiled. "It's the best."

"Why?"

"The students keep me honest. Every day I have to give a hundred percent. If I don't, they notice. I like the challenge. When there's a change—some kind of progress—it's the greatest feeling in the world. I know I've made an impact and it can last for a lifetime. I don't know of anything more rewarding than that."

His steady blue gaze never left her face. "Why special education?"

"Actually, that was an accident. When I was getting my master's I did some student teaching. My paperwork got mixed up with someone else's and I ended up in a special ed class. Within two days, I was hooked. I changed my emphasis, took a few more classes and here I am. I started out working with kids who were deaf, then a couple of years ago I was switched to kids who have learning disabilities. Last year most had minor disabilities. Some had Down syndrome."

"How do you find the patience?"

She shrugged. "I just do. I adore them. Don't get me wrong, some of the kids can be really difficult, but most of them are determined to make it in the world. They want to be like everyone else, and if that means working ten times as hard, they'll do it."

She leaned toward him. "One of my students, Bryce, really wanted to learn to play the piano. It was going to be his grandmother's seventieth birthday and he wanted to surprise her by playing her favorite song. He practiced every day for two hours. While the other kids were out playing games, he was at the piano. It took him nearly three months, but he mastered it. I was lucky enough to be there for the birthday celebration. He was so proud of himself. His grandmother was stunned and we were all pretty much in tears.''

''Your eyes light up when you talk about the kids,'' he said. ''They're lucky to have you.''

She chuckled. ''I know this is going to sound like a cliché, but I'm lucky to have them.'' Her humor faded. ''I won't pretend it's easy. There are tough times. Kids don't always make the progress I'd hope they would. Parents can be difficult—either expecting too much or not enough. Some parents can't see their children as anything but flawed and broken. Then there's the school system itself. We're constantly fighting for money and resources.''

''Any favorite students?''

The question caught her off guard and made her think of Eva. Not today, she told herself. Not right now.

''Teachers aren't supposed to have favorites.''

''But you do.''

''Sometimes,'' she admitted.

''Do you ever need a break?''

''Sure. That's why I'm here. My friend Cassie offered me the use of the family summer house for a month and I jumped at the chance. I want to be as lazy as possible, doing nothing so I can recharge my energy.''

''I remember Cassie,'' he said. ''Wasn't she your maid of honor at the wedding?''

''That's her.''

Rick listened and watched as Mandy brought him up-to-date on some other people he'd known through her. She still used her hands when she talked, gesturing broadly and moving her body. He laughed at the funny bits and asked questions, all the while observing the play of emotion on her face.

Her wide, green eyes kept very few secrets. In them he saw affection for Cassie, just as he'd seen love for her students a few minutes ago, along with a flash of some darker emotion. Something that disturbed her. A man, he wondered? Someone who didn't share her dreams?

His mother hadn't said that Mandy was involved with anyone serious, but then his mother was very careful to pick and choose her information as it suited her best. Besides, it wasn't as if he ever grilled his mother about Mandy. Until she'd called and suggested lunch, he hadn't thought he would ever see her again.

The waitress returned, but he sent her away, asking for a little more time.

"You still live in Los Angeles, don't you?" he asked.

"Torrance," she said. "It's a nice area. Close to the beach, without the beach prices."

"Not exactly Beverly Hills," he teased. "Do you still get over there for shopping?"

"Not on a teacher's salary."

"No credit cards from Daddy?"

She laughed. "He tries. Every time we get together, he hands me an American Express card, but I keep saying no. It's bad enough that my Christmas and birthday presents are things like living-room furniture or a new car."

"Most people wouldn't complain."

"I'm not complaining. Not exactly. But I do like to think that I'm making it on my own."

"You're his only child."

"I don't know. Some of his girlfriends could qualify."

Her eyes sparkled with humor as she spoke. Rick recalled his ex-father-in-law's preference for young, leggy blondes.

"Are they your age now?" he asked.

"Oh, yeah. A couple have been younger. At least we can swap clothes." She laughed. "He's currently dating the star of his last art film, so she's about thirty-two. I know eventually he's going to start going out with the female leads from his teen films. Then I don't know what I'm going to do."

She picked up her glass and took a sip. "I'm ragging on him, but the truth is he's a terrific father. He gets caught up in his work, but I know he cares about me a lot."

Martin Carter was a successful movie producer who had been responsible for some of the most successful, high-class films ever produced. He also had a soft spot for teen slasher movies. The combination made for interesting cocktail parties.

"I saw his last one. *Autumn Hills,*" he said.

Mandy looked at him. Her full mouth quivered slightly. "An elegantly made picture with a true, visionary ending."

"Yeah, I didn't get it, either."

She laughed. "I sat there, staring at the screen thinking, is it me? I can't believe how much money that thing made. I kept feeling like it was a modern version of 'The Emperor's New Clothes.' No one was willing to admit he or she didn't get the story." She sighed. "My father, the artist."

"At least he doesn't try to manipulate his children."

Mandy's smile broadened. "You wouldn't be referring to your mother, would you?"

"Me? Never."

"Uh-huh. She sure twisted me around this time. I was really surprised by her suggestion that I call you so we could meet for lunch."

"Yet you obeyed."

"That I did."

He looked at her pretty face, at her shining red curls, at the slight hint of cleavage at the scoop of her dress. He thought of the pleasure he felt in seeing her again, and the not-so-subtle sexual energy humming between them.

"I'm not sorry you called," he said.

"Me, either."

They stared at each other. Rick felt a definite heat flare between them. Her hand lay on the table and he wanted to reach out to put his on top. He wanted to trace the pale blue veins on the inside of her wrist and feel the gentle pulse of her heartbeat at the curve of her neck. He wanted a lot of things.

The growing desire surprised him. Mandy had always been attractive and he'd expected to still find her so, but he hadn't thought there would be this...*wanting*.

She hadn't been his first lover, but she had been his first serious girlfriend. He'd loved her with all his inept heart had been capable of. As for their sex life, he didn't remember very much except that he'd been young and had had unlimited access to a willing female for the first time in his life. He winced as he recalled being far more interested in quantity than quality. He doubted Mandy's memories of the events were as good his own.

"What are you thinking?" she asked. "You have the most interesting expression on your face."

"Just taking a little trip down memory lane."

"Want to share?"

That he'd probably been a lousy lover when they'd been married? "I don't think so."

It wasn't exactly lunch conversation. Nor was the fact that he knew a whole lot more about pleasing a woman these days. It seemed unlikely he would have the opportunity to show Mandy what he'd learned, although the idea intrigued him.

"Oh, come on, Rick. After all this time, we can't possibly have any secrets worth keeping."

The waitress returned, relieving him of the necessity of answering.

"You two ready to order?"

Mandy sighed. "I suppose we can't keep the table all day." She flipped open her menu. "I'll have the California chicken salad."

He didn't bother looking at the selections. "I'll have the same."

The waitress wrote down their order and left.

Mandy stared at him, wide-eyed. "You? Eating a salad? On purpose? But you hate vegetables, and lettuce makes you gag."

"You're exaggerating."

"Maybe a little, but I still remember the fuss you made when I had the audacity to serve both a salad and green beans with a meal. The way you went on about eating two vegetables in the same meal has stayed with me forever."

He winced slightly. "Not exactly the urban image I wanted to cultivate. I was a kid when we got married."

"So was I." She shrugged. "I guess that was part of the problem. I always thought that liking each other, as well as loving each other, should have been enough. But it wasn't."

"From this distance, it's a lot easier to see what went wrong. But back then, it was complicated and confusing."

Mandy nodded.

Rick hadn't thought about their marriage in forever. For the first time in years, he had a twinge of regret. Mandy was right. Liking and loving each other should have been enough.

"Okay, no long faces," she said firmly. "If this conversation turns serious again, I'm going to torment you with my vast knowledge of knock-knock jokes. They're very popular with the elementary school set."

"That will keep me in line."

She grinned. "Don't mess with me, mister, or I'll give you a time-out."

"You have to realize I know next to nothing about robots," Rick was saying an hour later. "However we all give input on large projects. The philosophy is that even if it's not an area of expertise, we can all see the big picture."

"I get that part," Mandy said. "But what I don't understand is the whole housecleaning robot thing. The guy can't have been serious."

"He was. His company had already invested every penny they had. They needed more funding to take it to the next level, and we were their best option for a source. The foundation offers all kinds of grants and loans for innovation."

He pushed away his salad. Neither of them had eaten much. It was far more interesting to talk. Mandy kept thinking that if she and Rick had had this much fun together while they'd been married, they would never have split up.

"So we built a mock-up of a house. Just the interior—a few basic rooms. We furnished it, added some dust and let the robot go."

"And?"

He shrugged. "It did great. Dusted, vacuumed, even moved a glass vase without breaking it."

"So when can I expect this wonder at my local discount store?"

"You can't. I got the bright idea to add a dog to the equation."

Mandy blinked at him. "Why?"

"Many households have a pet. Dogs and cats are the most common. Plus the dog was handy. One of the guys on our staff brings one to work with him every day. What I really wanted was a kid, but we didn't have one of those hanging around."

"Pity," she said, managing not to smile. "You could have tried at one of the local schools."

"Naw. That would have taken too long. So I put the dog in the house with the robot."

"Why do I have a feeling this didn't go well?"

"Let's just say Mr. Robot didn't like pets. He started chasing the poor dog from room to room, trying to vacuum it. I finally rescued the dog and we had to pass on the robot project."

"So that guy really hates you."

"Probably," Rick said cheerfully. "I doubt that he's alone. I pass on far more projects than I approve."

He spoke with a confidence that had been missing all those years ago, Mandy thought. Being in charge looked good on him. But based on his new and improved body, she would guess that just about anything would look good on him.

"What happened to laser physics?" she asked. "I thought that was your life."

"It was…for a while. I enjoyed my work. I'd been smart enough to insist on patent ownership as part of my employment contract. I invented a fair amount while I was with the company. They have an exclusive license on more than half of my inventions, which makes them happy."

"And they pay well for the privilege, which makes you happy," she said. "Am I right?"

He nodded. "I've licensed the other patents out to different companies. The government is using a couple."

"Jo mentioned you were doing well financially."

"Mom likes to brag. I do okay. For now my work at the foundation is interesting. Eventually I'm probably going to go back into research, but only when I'm ready to head up my own facility."

"Still don't like being told what to do?"

"Does anyone?"

"Some people like being followers."

He eyed her. "Not you. As I recall, you were very big on being in charge."

"That's because I always knew best."

He chuckled. The waitress appeared and cleared their plates. After giving each of them a pointed look, she placed the check in the center of the table.

Rick grabbed it. Mandy held up her hands. "You've just finished telling me about your incredible success. I get by on a teacher's salary, with the occasional expensive gift from my father. Don't expect me to fight you for the check."

"Fair enough."

He leaned toward her, resting his forearms on the table. "This is nice," he told her.

She knew what he meant—them sitting together and talking. She didn't know what he was feeling, but she'd been all tingly ever since spotting him. As reunions went, this one was darned nice.

"I'm glad we got together," she said. "We should have done it a long time ago."

He nodded, then stunned her by stretching out his arm and resting his hand on top of hers. "I'm sorry, Mandy. About the way we parted and how the marriage ended. It wasn't my finest hour."

"Mine, either. But let's not spoil the afternoon by talking about that." She glanced at her watch and was stunned to see they'd been sitting there for over two hours. "It's getting late. What time do you have to be back at the office?"

"I don't."

"Really?" She shifted her attention to the ocean below. It would be a pity for this to end so quickly. "What I would really like to do is walk along the beach by the edge of the water. Get my toes wet. Want to join me?"

He turned to study the crowded beach. "Sure, but I have a modification to make on your suggestion."

She pretended to shiver. "Oh, honey, I just love when you talk like a scientist."

He laughed. "Okay. How would you feel about taking your toe-wetting walk along a private beach instead of this one?"

She groaned. ''Let me guess. The private beach is all yours, compliments of the patent licenses we just talked about.''

''You game?''

Spend more time with Rick on a private beach that he owned? Gee, what a tough decision.

''Lead the way.''

After paying the bill, Rick escorted Mandy out to the parking lot. He gave her cursory instructions, his cell number and promised to drive slow.

Ten minutes later they were on Highway 101, heading north. Mandy kept her Volvo—a gift from her father two years ago—a safe distance behind Rick's flashy sports car. No doubt he could have driven circles around her, but he didn't show off. Although he had taken the time to lower the convertible top.

She figured his car cost more than she'd made in the past two years combined. Laser physics paid well when one was at the top of one's game.

They exited north of Santa Barbara, circling under the highway and heading toward the ocean. The two-lane road offered occasional glimpses of the water. A mile later, they turned onto a private drive, which led to another. By the fifth turn, Mandy was completely confused.

Rick drove into a brick driveway, passing a tall stucco fence surrounding what looked like a massive estate. They drove for nearly a minute before she saw the house.

The three-story structure took her breath away. She had a brief impression of elegance and a remodeling project in progress, then the driveway curved and she had a perfect view of the ocean.

Rick pulled up in front of the house, and Mandy stopped behind him. Tall trees offered shade, while lush plants blossomed and trailed over the grounds. Talk about paradise.

She stepped out of her car, not sure where to look first. The house was compelling, but so was the ocean.

"Okay," she said, walking toward him. "I'm impressed. It's amazing."

"Thanks."

She hoped he would offer to show her the house, but he didn't, instead turning toward the water and leading the way to a worn path. It led to a low bluff, which in turn had stairs down to the beach.

Mandy followed him to the sand, where she paused to slip off her sandals. As she lifted one foot, she nearly lost her balance. He put out an arm to steady her. When she was barefoot, he pulled off his shoes and socks, then took her hand in his and started for the water.

Their fingers laced together in a familiar embrace. Mandy stumbled slightly, but not because the ground was uneven. Instead she found herself oddly confused and wondering why, after all this time, holding Rick's hand felt so very right.

Chapter Three

"How long have you lived here?" Mandy asked.

"About a year. It's a great house, but it's old and the previous owners didn't do much to keep it updated, or even in good repair. I've been having some work done, and doing some myself."

She glanced at him and smiled. "Ooh, a handyman. My personal fantasy."

He knew she was teasing, and that her words didn't mean anything, but her saying "fantasy" made his blood pressure spike. What was it about being with Mandy? Why did his body react so strongly to her?

On a purely intellectual basis he could appreciate that she was attractive. She was a nice person, funny, passionate. These were generic qualities that always appealed to him. He had also already been physically intimate with Mandy. He knew what she looked like naked, and how she responded. Perhaps that knowledge fueled his already active imagination.

All good information, he told himself wryly, but for once his brain couldn't explain exactly why he was acting the way he was. There was just some…chemistry between them. He should enjoy it and stop trying to analyze it.

The sand was warm under his bare feet. The light breeze teased at his clothes. Blue, blue ocean stretched out for as far as the eye could see. While he knew all the reasons the water was the color it was, and why that color changed so many times during a day, right now he didn't want to think about light, refraction, current, or even electrons. He just wanted to be.

"I don't do this enough," he said, gazing at the view and enjoying the feel of Mandy's hand pressed against his own. "I promised myself, when I bought the place, that I would spend time down here by the water. Somehow that got lost."

She sighed. "Isn't that always the way? I live on a little hill with a minor view. When I was first in the house, I would sit on the balcony and watch the sunset, followed by the lights in town coming on. It was pretty and very relaxing. But in a matter of weeks, it became commonplace. Why does that always happen?"

He glanced at her, momentarily caught up in her green eyes. "Do you really want the psychological explanation or are you just making conversation?"

She laughed. "What do you think?"

"That you are more lovely than I remember. I'm trying to figure out if I have a faulty memory, or if you've become more beautiful."

Her breath caught in her throat. "Wow. That was really good. You used to fumble over telling me my dress looked nice. You've been practicing your compliments."

"I've learned to say what I think," he corrected, angling himself so he stood in front of her.

Slowly, so she could pull away if she wanted to, he brought up his free hand and lightly traced the curve of her cheek. Soft skin, he thought. Soft, warm and very appealing. He tucked her hair behind her ear and stared into her eyes.

This close he could see the different shades of green that made up her irises. Her pupils dilated slightly.

His overdeveloped intellect instantly began pumping out information about the possible causes of that dilation. As the sun continued to shine brightly in the sky, the most likely cause was sexual arousal. Scientifically—

Shut up, Rick told his brain, turning his attention to Mandy's full mouth. Her breathing had increased, but then so had his. Doing what he was thinking of doing was several different kinds of crazy. It was also irresistible.

He lowered his head until he could press his mouth against hers. The soft kiss should have been pleasant. He didn't remember much about what had happened before when he'd kissed her, so he had only minor expectations. He was unprepared to be swept away.

The instant skin contacted skin, his body heat flared. Need roared through him with the subtlety of a laser beam cutting through metal. Blood bubbled, boiled, then pooled in points south, and all this with the lightest of pressure.

He angled his head slightly and pressed a little more firmly. She responded by leaning into him. Somehow they weren't holding hands anymore. His were on her waist and hers rested on his shoulders. He took a step closer, or maybe she did, he wasn't sure. There was too much data for him to…

The hell with it, he thought, consciously turning off his brain and feeling the moment. They pressed together, straining slightly, both greedy for more. He was intimately aware of her soft breasts pressing into his chest. His fingers twitched slightly as he thought of sliding higher and touching her there. Cupping her, teasing her nipples until they were as hard and ridged as he was.

Instead he concentrated on her mouth. He licked her lower lip. The sweet taste of her stunned him into licking it again, then gently drawing her lip into his mouth and sucking. Pulsing need grew with each nanosecond of contact. When she parted, he didn't need a second invitation to sweep inside.

At the first brush of her tongue, a thrill shot through him. His arousal throbbed as more and more blood rushed into already engorged flesh. He wrapped his arms around her, pulling her closer still, wanting them to meld into one symbiotic being.

He felt her hands on his back. They moved up and down, making him wish she touched bare skin. The kiss deepened and became more frantic. The impulse to lower her to the ground and take her right there nearly overwhelmed him. He was as sexually out of control as he'd ever been.

The realization stunned him, then brought with it a measure of control. He eased away from her and broke the kiss. Slowly he opened his eyes.

The flush of arousal on her face nearly did him in. Her eyes were wide and unfocused, her lips damp, parted and swollen. He could see the fluttering pulse at the base of her neck and didn't doubt that he displayed all the same symptoms. Plus one more that was damn painful.

The rush of the ocean drowned out the sound of their rapid breathing, but he could see the rise and fall of her chest, along with the hint of tight nipples under her dress and bra.

She blinked a couple of times, then asked, "Who are you?"

He chuckled. She didn't.

"I'm serious, Rick. That was incredible. I don't remember passion like that before, do you?"

"No."

"I wonder what's different."

His brain kicked back in, offering several logical, scientific explanations. He ignored them. "*We're* different."

She drew in a deep breath. "I guess so. At least you are. You're polished and charming, a great kisser."

She lowered her arms to her side and stepped back, forcing him to release her waist.

Her gaze narrowed. "You're also smart, rich and successful. Why are you still single?"

He'd heard the compliments before. But somehow they meant more coming from Mandy. He shrugged.

A boat moved through the ocean, the loud engine causing them both to turn and watch the craft's progress. They were close and somehow it seemed right to slip his arm around Mandy's waist. She leaned against him.

Need still filled him, but he had a little more control now. However, a distraction would be nice. He eyed the ocean. A *cold* distraction would be best.

"What about putting your toes in the water? There it is." He swept out his arm to include the whole beach.

"No splashing," she insisted as they walked toward the shore.

"You're such a girl."

She smiled up at him. "It's one of my best qualities."

He thought about holding her in his arms and kissing her. "I'd have to agree."

Talk about a pretty darned perfect moment, Mandy thought as they joined hands and walked down to the edge of the water. Every single cell in her body was still on full alert after Rick's amazing kiss. Just recalling the feel of his hard body against her was enough to get her heart thumping at about a hundred miles an hour. No one had ever made her feel so alive and aware with just a simple kiss.

They stepped into the surf. The cold water raced over her feet and up to her ankles. The contrast from the warm air and sand made her shriek, but it did nothing to quell the lingering heat inside her. It was as if her body temperature had been cranked up a few degrees. Her skin felt tight, her thighs ached, as did other more…*private* areas.

"Mandy?"

"Yes?"

"Does Cassie's beach house have a view?"

She blinked at him. From the tone of his voice, he'd asked the question before, but she hadn't heard him. It actually took her a second to put it all together. Her first instinct was to say "Cassie who?"

Then she remembered. Cassie Brightwell—her best friend for over fifteen years.

Rick pulled her out of the water. "Come on. We need to go sit down."

"You think?"

They walked up to the patio at the rear of the house. The weathered redwood deck held a white wrought-iron table-and-chair set, with a freestanding umbrella. There was a built-in brick BBQ in the corner, along with a gas grill. Tile countertops connected the two, and on the far end was a space to drop in a cooler. Talk about a nice setup.

"I thought Cassie's family's summer house was nice, but it's nothing compared to this."

Rick shrugged but didn't say anything. Mandy wasn't surprised. He might be content to enjoy his success, but he would never brag about it. Add that to his list of good qualities, which brought her back to her earlier question. Why wasn't he married?

She didn't have an answer and he hadn't been prepared to offer one. To be honest, she found herself not really minding that he wasn't married.

That realization made her uncomfortable so she plopped down on one of the chairs and shifted to a more neutral topic.

"Cassie needs a vacation as much as I do," she said.

Rick sat next to her. She gazed at him. The man was sure easy on the eyes.

"Why? Is she all right?"

Mandy waved a hand. "She was engaged. One day

she came home from work early and found Mr. Right in bed with her roommate. It was pretty horrible.''

Rick frowned. "How's she handling it?"

"Better than I would. She's been in Arizona for a while. She quit her job and is moving back to L.A. She's joining me my last two weeks at the house and we're committed to some serious recreation. You know, reading trashy novels, eating plenty of chocolate, going to the latest chick flicks."

"Sounds like fun." He practically winced as he spoke.

"You're not much of a liar, are you?"

"No. I've never been good at that."

It was, she considered, yet another quality to put in the plus column.

"I haven't seen Cassie since the wedding," he said. "I remember you and I would double-date with her when we visited here."

Mandy nodded. Back when they'd all been a lot younger. "She went to college here while I went up north."

Stanford, she thought. Where her father had gone. Where she'd met Rick. "I remember thinking it was so cool how we got together. That it would make a good story when we were old."

"I ran into you. Literally."

"I know. I thought it was cute."

He frowned. "I was a klutz."

"You were charming and very into your work. I liked that."

"At first."

She sighed. "Yeah. At first." She didn't want to think about that. Instead she turned her attention to the house rising up behind them. "This place is huge. Does it echo when you walk around?"

His frown faded. "Sometimes. I'm thinking of hiring some people to stay here with me. To make the place more lived in."

"If I worked closer, I'd volunteer. It's beautiful."

"Come on. I'll give you the nickel tour."

He started to stand up, then fell back into his seat with an exasperated shake of his head. "Excuse me," he said, and pulled a small pager out of his pocket. He read the screen. The frown returned. "I have to make a quick call to the office. Give me a second."

After pulling a tiny cell phone from his pocket, he hit a single button and leaned back in his chair. "Benson," he said curtly.

He listened for a minute, then glanced at his watch. "I'm not making the meeting, Clara. You'll have to reschedule it." He looked at Mandy and winked. "No. I'm not coming back to the office today. Please reschedule everything for me."

He held the phone away from his ear. Mandy could hear someone talking very fast. Rick waited it out.

"You're right. I should have called. Uh-huh. Yes. You can punish me when next you see me. Talk to you later."

With that he pushed another button and tucked the small cell phone back into his shirt pocket.

Mandy sprang to her feet. "I've been keeping you."

"And I've enjoyed being kept." He rose and moved close. "Don't go there," he told her. "I'm a big boy and I made the decision to stay with you because I wanted to. I work about a sixty-hour week. I've more than earned an afternoon off."

"But your meeting."

"They'll survive without me."

She wasn't completely convinced, but his work schedule wasn't her problem. "If you work such long hours, when do you find time to practice your scuba diving?"

"I work hard, then I play hard. I've learned to focus on whatever the task is at hand and not worry about anything else."

Intensity radiated from him. She thought about his focus when he'd kissed her. Yet another trait for the plus column.

"Do you need to get back for anything?" he asked.

"No."

Somehow nothing else seemed very important just now.

"Then let's take that tour," he said, holding out his hand.

The house was amazing. High ceilings and large windows added a feeling of light and space to every room. Old, worn pavers covered the main floor. Rick rubbed at a tile with his bare foot.

"I should probably replace these," he said. "But I like how the color has faded with time. You can see where people have walked before."

They crossed into a formal dining room. "This table was originally built for the house. I bought it from the previous owners."

The table in question was huge, made of thick planks of worn oak. It could easily seat fourteen. Two of the walls held arched glass doors that opened out into a walled garden. Mandy walked to the closest one and pushed it open. Instantly she was enchanted by the strong scent of honeysuckle. Vines trailed over the walls and down to the garden. Small benches offered seating area, and the same reddish pavers covered the whole garden.

"It's wonderful," she said, not daring to think how much this house must have cost. Not that Rick couldn't afford it, but still he'd come a long way from their small one-bedroom apartment in Boston.

"If I ever decide to entertain, I thought it would be fun to set up a buffet inside, on the table, then have everyone eat out here."

She nodded, already able to visualize how it would be. Twinkling lights in the trees, lit torches in the corners, the call of the night creatures, and the honeysuckle perfuming the air while the sound of the surf provided background music.

She turned back to him. "The house is worth it just for this alone."

"I agree, but there's more."

He led the way into the remodeled kitchen. Stainless steel appliances gleamed against the granite countertop. There was an extradeep double sink, along with a separate vegetable sink at one end of the center island. A small table for four sat by the bay window opposite the entrance to the dining room.

"I eat in here," he said, "when I bother to eat at home."

She laughed. "Let me guess. Frozen dinners and cereal."

He shrugged sheepishly. "Okay. I've learned how to install cabinets and refinish a wood floor, but I'm not big on cooking."

They circled around to a large living room, then back to the entryway that was about the size of the first floor of her house. A fully stocked wine cellar had been tucked under the stairs.

"A new hobby," Rick admitted. "I'm currently collecting a whole lot more than I'm drinking. That could become a problem."

"Don't wines keep?"

"Some."

He started up the stairs.

Mandy followed, taking in the soaring ceilings, the elegant artwork, the hand-carved stair rail. The second-floor landing led to a large open family room, complete with enough television technology to stock an electronics store. Four remotes were lined up on the coffee table in front of a navy leather sofa.

"I don't want to know," she said.

Rick grinned. "If you think this is bad…"

He walked down the hall and opened the door on his left. She stepped into some kind of lab with equipment that beeped and flashed. There were shelves filled with partially assembled projects, or maybe they were completely assembled. She couldn't tell. Computers hummed. Somewhere under a stack of papers a phone rang.

"If you ever can't sleep," Rick said, closing the door, "ask me to explain what's in there. That should put you out in about five seconds."

She laughed. "It's a date."

Poor choice of words, she thought as they looked at each other, then looked away. Or maybe not, because it reminded her.

"Speaking of dates," she said, after she cleared her throat. "I'm not stepping on anyone's toes by being here, am I?"

"No. I'm between lady friends. What about you?

Is there some burly Neanderthal lurking nearby who's going to want to use my head as a bowling ball?''

''I don't date Neanderthals.''

The next room was a guest room, complete with an en suite bathroom and a view of the ocean that left her breathless. Two more bedrooms were empty. Rick's office was at the end of the hall. It was much tidier than his lab, with only one computer on a desk. Several bookshelves lined two walls and a wooden file cabinet stood against another.

He closed that door and paused in front of another staircase.

Mandy started to ask what was upstairs. At the same moment she realized they hadn't seen his bedroom. Then the pieces clicked into place. Of course.

''The master is on the third floor?'' she asked.

He nodded. ''I took out a couple of walls, did some remodeling. There's a wraparound balcony and the view is terrific.''

''I'll bet.''

''Want to see?''

He hadn't asked her if she wanted to see any other rooms, and she had a feeling she knew why. None of the other rooms were…dangerous. But a bedroom. That was different.

Mandy moved to the stairs and started climbing slowly. Her heart began to pick up the pace a little. The added rhythm had nothing to do with the physical exertion and everything to do with her attraction to Rick. That kiss back at the beach had showed her the possibilities. If they went into his bedroom…

Nothing would happen, she told herself, thinking it was crazy. She didn't have sex with strangers. She'd done that once and it had left her feeling sick with herself for weeks. Not that Rick was a stranger. He wasn't. He was her ex-husband, which made contemplating any physical relationship completely crazy.

"I can hear you thinking from here," he said, moving behind her. "I'm showing you the house, Mandy, not kidnapping you for the sex trade."

She reached the third floor and moved away from the stairs. "Am I that easy to read?"

He stepped onto the landing and stared at her. "Maybe I remember what you were like."

"We've both admitted we're different."

"Not that different. Come on. You'll be perfectly safe."

Which was good news, right?

The master suite was just as fabulous as the rest of the house. Rick had set up a home gym in a small room at the back of the house. There were his-and-her-closets big enough to camp in, a tub built for eight or nine and a double-headed shower.

The bedroom itself faced the ocean, with the bed on a platform. The sleek, modern furniture fit surprisingly well in the old Spanish-style house. Sliding glass doors led out to the wraparound patio.

Mandy crossed to the glass and stepped outside. Warm sea air brushed against her skin. She could see to the ends of the world, or so it seemed. The grounds of the estate stretched out below, with the sea beyond.

"You've found a piece of paradise," she said.

He came up behind her and put a hand on her shoulder.

"So why aren't you dating a Neanderthal?" he asked.

The change of subject caught her off guard. "What?"

Rick shrugged. "Why aren't you dating someone? I'll ask you the same question you asked me. Why aren't you happily married with a bunch of kids?"

That wasn't exactly her question, but it was close enough. "I've learned it's better to be alone than to be with the wrong one."

His dark eyes flicked. "Ouch."

"I don't mean anything against you. We were young and impulsive." She waved her hand, not wanting to go into that right now. "There have been guys, but I've never felt that I was really in love. I could never see the relationship lasting more than a few months. When I do marry again, I want to get it right. I want it to be forever."

She could feel the weight of his hand on her shoulder. His fingers were warm and strong. An image of them sliding over her body made her shiver slightly.

"For what it's worth," she said through a suddenly tight throat, "I'm sorry it didn't work out for us."

"Me, too."

Was it her imagination, or was he moving closer? Or was she? Mandy could feel herself swaying slightly. The edges of the world seemed to blur a little bit until the only clear image she had was of Rick's face.

His hand moved down her arm to her waist. She felt a slight tug. Stepping toward him seemed the right thing to do.

They stared at each other.

"This is crazy," he murmured, his mouth blissfully close to hers. "I'm generally very cautious when it comes to a sexual relationship."

"Me, too. I really like to take things slow, get to know the person."

"Right. I'm sort of a two-months-later kind of guy." His mouth brushed against hers.

She caught her breath. "At least two months. Sometimes longer." She kissed him lightly, then drew her tongue along his bottom lip.

"Much longer," he whispered. "I have no idea what's going on between us, Mandy. It doesn't make any sense."

"Tell me about it."

"We should stop," he said, then kissed her jaw and nibbled her earlobe. "I'll stop. Any second now."

She ran her fingers through his thick hair and arched against him. He was already hard. Her most feminine place throbbed in response, swelling and readying.

"I'll stop, too," she told him as he moved back to her mouth. "Or maybe not."

Chapter Four

Telling herself this was a bad idea didn't seem to dampen Mandy's desire. Even as Rick kissed her more deeply, exploring her mouth and pulling her close, she felt herself straining for more. Little things like sense and rational thought didn't seem very important when compared with the heated passion flaring between them.

She'd never felt like this before. Never felt such an overpowering need to be physically intimate with someone. Every part of her ached. Her skin felt so sensitized that the lightest touch could bring her to her knees. She found herself wanting to rip off her clothes, to tear off his and have Rick and herself fall together in a tangle of arms and legs.

"Mandy," Rick breathed against her mouth.

He sounded out of breath, which made her shiver in delight, too. She wanted him unable to think, unable to breathe, unable to do anything but be with her right now.

With their arms around each other, still kissing, they began to move back into the bedroom. She felt the smooth hardwood floor against her bare feet. A memory flickered in her mind, that she'd left her purse and her shoes downstairs. Not that she was going to need either right now.

Rick cupped her face in his hands, then ran his fingers through her long hair. "You're so beautiful," he murmured as he rained kisses on her cheeks, her nose, her mouth before pressing his lips to the pulse point at the base of her throat. She clung to him to stay upright.

"Are you sure?" he asked. "I don't want to push you."

She gave a strangled laugh. Sure? She was sure she was going to die if they didn't make love right this second.

Rather than answer the question with something as silly as words, she reached for the buttons on his short-sleeved shirt and began unfastening them. He gave a low groan and shifted so he could reach behind her.

She felt her zipper being lowered past her waist to her hips. Then his hands were on her bare skin. He was warm and tender as he stroked the length of her spine. Her dress dropped a few inches but caught in the crook of her elbows. She straightened her arms long enough to let it fall to the floor.

He took a step back and jerked his partially unbuttoned shirt out of his waistband. His gaze fixed on her body, he shrugged out of his shirt and went to work on his slacks. As a rule Mandy wasn't comfortable being stared at while she was partially—or completely—undressed. But somehow with Rick it didn't matter. The pleasure in his eyes, the straining ridge of his arousal, all told her that he liked what he saw.

They came together again, this time touching each other everywhere. He fumbled for the clasp on her bra while she explored the thick muscles of his back. She ran her fingers through the light dusting of hair over his sculpted chest, then moved lower to narrow hips. He freed her bra and dropped it to the ground, then rested his hand on her left breast.

All thought fled from her brain. She could only feel the gentle touch of his fingers on her skin. He moved his thumb against her tight nipple and fire shot through her. She gasped.

There was a quick movement and she felt herself falling. They tumbled together onto the mattress, his body half-covering hers.

Their naked legs brushed together. She looked up into his blue eyes and saw an answering fire flickering there. Need tightened his mouth. His hand slipped from her breast to her hip and back, making a lazy circle. He lowered his mouth to hers and kissed her.

Familiar, she thought hazily. Familiar, yet different. The combination was unexpected and arousing. Some things were the same—the taste of him, the heat—but others were different. She felt tension increasing from his simple touches. Years before, arousal and climax had always been difficult for her, but not today. Not with him.

He moved his hand lower until he cupped her between her legs. Jolts of need made her cry out. He rubbed her through her silk panties and she could tell that she was wet and ready.

With one long elegant tug, he removed her last scrap of clothing, then slipped his hands through her damp curls. As if drawn by a beacon, he instantly found her point of pleasure and introduced himself with a gentle caress.

She closed her eyes and arched her head back. It was too good, she thought, barely able to keep breathing. He touched her with a sureness that made her relax. Every brush of his fingers was more perfect than the one before. Then she felt warm, moist heat on her breasts. As his hand moved below, he licked her sensitive nipples, then began to suck on them. The combination was impossible.

"Now!" she breathed as her release swept over her. She had no control, no will. The pleasure rolled through her, making her cling to him and silently beg for it to go on forever.

Eventually, though, the tingles faded and reality returned. She opened her eyes to find Rick staring down at her intently.

"That was incredible," he said quietly.

She had to clear her throat before she could speak. "Actually, that would be my line," she said.

"I want you," he murmured. "I want to be inside you. I want to bury myself so deep that you don't have a choice but to do that again."

His words made her tremble.

"Okay," she managed to say, already feeling her own need flaring to life again.

He stood and peeled off his briefs, then opened a nightstand drawer and pulled out a condom. When he turned around and she saw his arousal, her need increased. She, too, wanted him inside, filling her, making her lose control for a second time.

He applied the protection, then settled between her knees. Again she had the sensation of a blending of the familiar and unfamiliar. Then he was kissing her and nothing mattered but his mouth and the probing she felt at the apex of her thighs.

She reached down a hand to guide him inside her. He was large and thick and she had to stretch to accommodate him. But what could have been uncomfortable was only spectacular.

More, she thought, pulsing toward him. More and more and more and more.

He read her mind. As they kissed and clung to each other, he began to move in and out of her. Each stroke filled her, brushing against sensitized nerves that began to quake in anticipation. Tension grew. More. She wanted more. He moved faster. She brought up her legs and wrapped them around his hips, pulling him deeper inside. A strong pulsing began in her belly, then moved outward. She couldn't stop it or control it or do anything but feel the growing release as it swelled and blossomed.

"Yes," he murmured, breaking the kiss and staring into her eyes. "Do it for me."

The erotic request pushed her over the edge. Still watching him, knowing *he* watched her, she gave herself up to the pleasure. Wave after wave of release rumbled through her, making her hold on tight and cry out. He gritted his teeth, obviously restraining himself as long as he could. Then he gave a groan of surrender. One more strong thrust and he was still. She felt the muscles in his body tense, then release with a sigh.

* * *

When the aftershocks subsided, Rick rolled off the bed and disappeared into the bathroom to deal with the condom. Mandy watched him go, not sure if she was supposed to duck under the sheets or start dressing. He returned before she could make up her mind, and held out a hand.

Still not certain about what was expected of her, she let him pull her to her feet, then waited while he drew back the covers and motioned for her to slide in first. He settled next to her, drew her close and wrapped his arms around her.

"Like I said…incredible," he told her as he nuzzled her hair.

Mandy wasn't so quick to relax. She enjoyed being in his arms, and the sensual aftershocks of her multiple releases were very nice, but…

"I can't believe we did that," she said, before she could stop herself.

Rick smiled. "I'll agree with you on that."

"But you don't seem upset."

"Are you?"

"No. Not upset." But definitely something, she thought, feeling contented but very confused.

He touched her face, then rested his hand on her upper arm. "I'm sure there's a perfectly reasonable explanation," he said.

"Which is?"

He gave a shrug. "Lots of things. We have a past, we haven't seen each other in a long time. There are old emotions and new discoveries. That sort of thing."

"Uh-huh. This is where I inform you that I've met other people from my past and have managed to get through entire evenings without once thinking about making love with them.''

A smile tugged at the corner of his mouth. "We didn't just think about it."

"I got that."

"Face it, Mandy, you're an amazing woman. I can't remember ever being swept away by passion like that, but it was great."

"For me, too," she admitted. "I just feel weird about it. We were married. We got a divorce. After eight years we fell into bed together. Doesn't that strike you as strange?"

"A little." He shifted and shoved a couple of pillows against the headboard, then sat up. "Okay, a lot strange. Apparently there's still something between us."

"How is that possible? It's been a long time." She sat up and sat cross-legged, facing him, with the sheet carefully pulled up to cover her breasts…not to mention the rest of her.

"Things didn't end well," he reminded her. "Maybe this is about working through that."

She might not have a Ph.D. in some scientific field, but even she could figure out that the fact they'd ended their marriage badly didn't explain having sex now.

"Try another one."

"Don't dismiss the idea," he said. "We fought, we disappeared from each other's lives. Maybe we should talk about what went wrong in our marriage."

"Now?" Was he serious? "We're both naked."

"So we can flash each other as a distraction if things get uncomfortable."

Mandy couldn't help laughing. "You're crazy,"

she said, wondering when Rick had changed so much. When they'd been married, talking about anything remotely touchy-feely had sent him screaming out of the room. Now he was suggesting it.

"Probably," he agreed with far too much cheer. "I'll even start."

He adjusted one of the pillows and frowned slightly. She waited, more than willing for him to go first.

"Okay. I was emotionally immature," he said. "You weren't my first lover, but you were my first girlfriend."

She stared at him. "What? You never told me that before."

"I was twenty-two. It wasn't something I liked to brag about."

"But…how is that possible?"

"Mandy, I was a total nerd. I didn't know how to talk to girls. I hadn't stopped growing and I was still tripping over my own feet." He shrugged again. "Which is off the point. I wanted to play house rather than have a mature relationship. I was more into sex being available than worrying about your needs. I wanted a mistress and a housekeeper to fulfill my vague fantasies of what marriage should be like. I was young and dumb and I'm sorry."

His ease of conversation didn't dilute his sincerity. She hadn't expected them to discuss their marriage at all, but if she had, she would never have thought Rick would be so willing to take responsibility for his part in things. She knew then that she couldn't do any less.

"I was young, too. Young and foolish with a lot of unrealistic expectations." She tucked the covers under her arms. "I used to watch my dad with all the women in his life. I don't remember how he was with my mom before she died, but after, he treated his girlfriends like pets or toys. They were easily discarded. I always wanted to be more than that. I wanted to be…everything to the man in my life.''

Rick winced. ''That was probably the one thing I didn't want you to be.''

''I know. You had your studies, which took up so much time. I wanted you to focus on me, and I wasn't willing to go find other interests. I didn't make friends, I didn't continue going to college.''

''We moved across the country,'' he reminded her. ''You were all alone.''

''Making excuses for me?'' she asked with a smile.

''Trying to see both sides.''

''I do that, too. With that pesky wisdom of hindsight, I know now that I should have gotten a life of my own instead of expecting you to be everything to me. If I'd had my own friends and things to do, I wouldn't have spent so much time waiting for you to come home. I wouldn't have resented your long hours, the study groups, the dinners with your professors.''

''Then I dragged in late, wanting sex rather than conversation. I'm sorry, Mandy.''

''Me, too.'' She sighed. ''The harder I tried to pull you to me, the more you pushed back. I felt you slipping away and I didn't know what to do.''

He nodded. ''Instead of talking about what was wrong, I ignored it, and you. I think we both wanted the other to give in, so we could each be right.''

She tilted her head and studied him. ''For a scientific nerd type, you know a lot about people.''

''I've learned some. I'm still learning. Light par-

ticles make a whole lot more sense to me, though.''
He shifted so he was lying on his side, facing her. ''I
remember the first time I saw you. I took one look
into those pretty green eyes and knew you were the
one. What happened to that?''

His question made her sad. She hadn't been the
one…not for him. He'd let her go without a backward
glance. Of course, she'd done the same with him.

''It got lost,'' she said.

''Too many maybes,'' he told her. ''Maybe if I'd
responded to your needs better. Maybe if you'd fit in
to our life in Boston more. Maybe, maybe, maybe.''

''And now everything is different.''

So different, she thought. She'd finally figured out
how to make her life work. If she'd stayed with Rick,
would that have happened? So many things would
have been different. She might never have found her
way into her current teaching position. She might
never have met Eva.

''What?'' he asked. ''I saw something in your eyes.
Something I can't explain.''

''Eva,'' she said, knowing right away what he
meant. ''I was thinking that if you and I had stayed
together, my life would be really different. I wouldn't
have met her.''

''Who is she?''

''A little girl in my class. She's eight. She's one
of the kids with Down syndrome. She'll never have
a regular life like everyone else, but I see so much
potential in her. She's a sweet spirit slowly being
crushed to death in foster care. Her parents were both
kids on the street. Her mother was into drunks. We
think her father was killed in a drive-by shooting.
Eva's been in and out of foster care for years. Her

mother kept taking her back, then abandoning her. A few months ago, Eva was made a ward of the state.''

Mandy recited facts, but Rick could easily see past them. ''What are you waiting for?'' he asked. ''Or have you already started the adoption procedure.''

Mandy looked surprised. ''Is it that obvious?''

''It is to me.''

She sighed. ''The situation is complicated. If I adopted her, I would be a single mother. Eva deserves a lot of individual attention. How much would I be able to give her, working all the time?''

''Wouldn't your schedules be similar?''

''Most of the time. But not all of it. There are some financial issues, too. My dad has offered to help, but I hate the idea of sponging off him. It's a big step and I'm trying to figure out if it's one I'm prepared to take on my own.''

Earlier he'd asked if there was anyone special in her life. Now Mandy had confirmed she was alone. Rick couldn't figure out why some guy hadn't snapped her up years ago. She was pure fantasy material. Even though they'd just made love, knowing that she was less than two feet away, and naked, made him hard.

But it was more than sex, he told himself. He enjoyed talking to her. Being around her. Why wouldn't she be chasing off men with a stick?

''Why have you been avoiding Mr. Right?'' he asked.

''He's been avoiding me.'' Her mouth twisted. ''You would be amazed how fast men can run when someone mentions the phrase 'special-needs child.'''

''Why?'' he asked, knowing the situation would create challenges, but not clear on why they would be a deal breaker. "Are you saying with Eva you wouldn't want children of your own?"

"Of course not. I think both would be great, but so far I haven't had a lot of offers. Most of the men I've met are only interested in 'perfect' children. Those who don't qualify need not apply."

She sounded bitter, and he couldn't blame her. While adopting Eva sounded like what she wanted to do, it wouldn't be easy, whether or not she was alone.

He tried to reconcile the thoughtful adult sitting in his bed with the volatile young woman he'd married.

"I'm impressed with all that you've done," he said lightly. "Next you'll be telling me that you've taken up a hobby or two yourself."

She flipped her hair over her shoulders. "I'll have you know that I not only crochet, I hike. I even camp on occasion."

"You? Camp? Where do you plug in your electric curlers?"

She grabbed the free pillow and threw it at him. "I do without for those days."

"I'm even more impressed."

She raised her eyebrows. "I've been horseback riding, too. I've taken Eva a few times and she loves it."

The longing was back in her eyes. He wanted to tell her to just go for it—that everything would work out fine. But time and experience had taught him that saying the words didn't make anyone a believer. Nor did they change the situation. Mandy would have to figure out what to do on her own.

If only he'd known this much about life and people eight years ago, he thought, things might not have ended so badly.

"I'm sorry," he said, reaching out his hand and capturing her fingers.

"For what?"

"Before. How it ended. My part in that. I know back then I made a big case about not technically doing anything wrong. I've learned since then. The problem wasn't with what I did or didn't do, it was about disconnecting from the marriage."

Mandy squeezed Rick's fingers, then released them. So they were going to talk about *that,* she thought, not sure if she wanted to.

"Maybe we shouldn't go there," she whispered, but it was too late.

The memories returned in vivid detail and blinding color. Of the silence in the hallway of their apartment building. Of the melting snow dampening the hem of her jeans. She had hated winter in Boston, hated the snow and the cold. She'd walked into their tiny apartment to find coats on the sofa. Not just Rick's coat, but another one…an unfamiliar one.

Her heart had stopped. She remembered that distinctly. The sensation of a steady beating in her chest, followed by nothing. Not even a flutter.

Knowing she shouldn't, yet unable to stop herself, she'd entered the small bedroom. The room was so tiny that the bed took up most of the floor space. Their battered dresser was in the living room by the bookcase.

Mandy told herself to breathe slowly, that the past didn't matter. But suddenly she was there again. Staring at Rick, a younger Rick, kissing another woman. Touching her. They were both still dressed, but with their lips locked and his hand on her breast, it was pretty clear where things were going.

"Mandy?"

She tried to shake off the memories. "It was a long time ago," she said.

"Not long enough." He stared at her face. "Does it still bother you?"

"Not in the way that you mean. I'm not hurt or anything."

How could she explain there were lingering shards of her shattered life stabbing her soul? The ghosts weren't as much about him or her but about what should have been and what was.

Suddenly she was very aware of being naked. She hated to get out from under the protection of the covers, but there didn't seem to be any other way to reach her clothes. She sucked in a breath and stood, then circled around the bed, picking up panties and her bra as she went.

"What are you doing?" he asked.

"It's getting late."

"I thought you didn't have other plans for the day."

"I don't. It's just…" She pulled her dress up over her hips. "I really need to get going."

Rick watched her without speaking. His serious gaze spoke volumes for him, though. She zipped up her dress and searched for her shoes before remembering she'd left them downstairs. She faced him and crossed her arms over her chest.

"What?" she asked.

"Why does it have to end like this?"

"Like what?"

He shook his head. "It doesn't matter."

But it did. She couldn't explain her compulsion to

leave. After all that had happened, she felt unsettled. Time and distance would ease that.

"You haven't changed as much as I thought," he said flatly, not bothering to get up and get dressed. "After all these years, you still run when things get tough."

His words cut through her…probably because she didn't have a good defense.

"You call this tough?" she asked, motioning to the bed. "In my mind, it was too easy. I don't have a clue as to what happened today. One minute I was minding my own business, the next Jo suggested I contact you for lunch. Somehow we ended up in bed. Doesn't any part of that strike you as strange?"

"I don't know. Maybe."

"Well, it does for me. We shouldn't have done this. The sex…" What about the sex? It had been great, but what had she been thinking? Or not thinking? She and Rick were strangers.

"I have to go," she repeated, and headed out the door.

As she ran down the steps she half expected him to come after her. He didn't. Rick claimed she hadn't changed as much as he had thought. She could say the same about him. She might be the one who was running, but he'd always found it far too convenient to let her go.

Chapter Five

Mandy was still shaking when she arrived back at Cassie's beach house. It had taken her five tries to get from Rick's house to the highway; she'd been so upset, she'd turned north instead of south. What should have been about a thirty-minute trip had taken her nearly an hour.

But she was safe now, she told herself as she paced the length of the living room. Safe and everything would be fine. Eventually. She just had to figure out what had happened back there and how to put it in perspective. Oh, and she also had to find a place to put her growing anger.

The anger surprised her. After the past five or six hours she would have expected to be dealing with a lot of emotions, but why was she mad? Or was the anger simply a cover for some other feeling?

She didn't want to think about that, so she continued to pace and mutter and try to distract herself. Only her brain kept flashing back to her time with Rick. She could recall dozens of things he'd said— how he'd smiled, the changes in his body and the way they'd been together in bed.

"Not that!" she said aloud. "It was a mistake. All of it. What should have been a charming, easy encounter with my ex turned into something…"

What? Horrible? Not exactly. Scary? Maybe. Confusing? Yes. Definitely confusing.

The phone rang. Mandy spun to face the plain beige instrument sitting on the counter dividing the kitchen from the living area. Her first instinct was to run. She didn't want to hear whatever Rick had to say. Then she reminded herself that not only did he *not* have her phone number, he'd never been very good on damage control or follow-up. He preferred to disappear until things blew over.

"Hello?" she said into the receiver.

"Hey, how's sunny Southern California?"

Mandy sagged against the counter. Relief filled her. Cassie. Just the person she needed to talk to.

"It's beautiful here," she said, pulling out a stool and settling on it. "August is always wonderful weather."

"I can't wait until I get to experience it myself."

"How's the transition?" Mandy asked.

Cassie worked in a hospital in Arizona. She'd recently given notice, causing her boss to panic and swear she couldn't survive without Cassie there.

"Slow. Really slow. I think they're hoping to entice me into staying here, but that's not going to happen."

Mandy nodded sympathetically. "How are you doing?"

It was more than a casual question. It hadn't been all that long since Cassie had walked in on her fiancé and roommate doing the wild thing. What was it about men and other women?

"Okay. Some days are easier than others. I'm working hard, which helps me forget. Maybe it will all crash in on me when I'm at the beach and don't have as many distractions."

"Maybe you'll find out that you didn't care about him as much as you thought."

"I can only hope." Cassie sighed. "Okay, enough about my pathetic life. What's going on there?"

Mandy didn't know what to say. How to explain the past few hours of her life.

"Oh, Mandy, it's not Eva, is it? Has something happened?"

"No. She's fine. At least she was a couple of days ago. I talked with Daisy, her foster mother, and she's enjoying the summer."

"Then what?"

"I'm stupid."

"That's not how I think of you, but okay."

Despite everything, Mandy smiled. "You weren't supposed to agree."

"But how could I help myself?" She chuckled. "Never mind. Why do you think you're stupid?"

"I had lunch with Rick."

The pause on Cassie's end was oddly satisfying, Mandy thought.

"Rick?" Cassie said, sounding stunned. "Your ex-husband Rick?"

"Uh-huh. He lives in Santa Barbara now, and when

Jo found out I was coming up here, she suggested we get together."

"How was it?"

Mandy found herself blinking away unexpected tears. "I don't know. At first it was great, but then everything sort of fell apart. I don't know what Jo was thinking. It's been eight years. Why would she want us to see each other? I guess she thought we had unfinished business or something, but as far as I'm concerned, it should have stayed unfinished."

No way was she going to mention that they'd made love.

"You sound angry," Cassie said.

"I am, which is crazy. I don't exactly know why, but I have a strong desire to start throwing things."

"Feel free to toss the couch. For the past three years I've been telling my folks we need to replace it."

Despite everything, Mandy smiled. "I'm not sure I could. It looks big."

"Suit yourself." Cassie cleared her throat. "Here's the thing. And you're not going to like it."

"I already don't."

Cassie laughed. "Listen first, complain later. Okay?"

"Sure."

"There's too much energy there, Mandy. Whatever happened between you and Rick should have been over a long time ago. The fact that he can push your buttons means that you're still connected in some way. Jo was right. You did need to see Rick so you could figure that out."

"I don't want to be connected to him," she said, even as she had a bad feeling Cassie might be right.

Why else would she, Mandy, have jumped into bed so quickly and easily? Why else would she now be so upset?

"I'm not sure you get a choice in the matter. But now that you know what the problem is, you can start to fix it."

Mandy didn't like the sound of that. Could she really have been stuck on her ex for all these years? "I'll have to think about it."

"Fine by me."

Mandy shifted the receiver to the other ear. "You forgot to say that he was a complete jerk and was never grateful enough that he was lucky enough to have been married to me."

Cassie laughed again. "That, too."

They talked for a few more minutes. When Mandy hung up, she felt marginally better...and marginally worse.

Connected to Rick? Was it possible? Surely time would have severed all the ties they had.

Yesterday Mandy would have staked her life on that fact, but now she wasn't so sure. Still restless, she walked into the kitchen and started cleaning already clean counters. She needed physical activity to release her pent-up energy. Maybe she should take a long walk on the beach. That would be a whole lot more fun than cleaning.

She put down her sponge, rinsed her hands, then headed upstairs to the bedroom she was using for her visit. The master suite had its own bath, while the other two bedrooms shared a Jack-and-Jill-style bathroom.

Mandy slipped out of her dress and pulled on shorts and a T-shirt. It took her a couple of minutes to brush her hair and secure it in a ponytail. After reapplying sunscreen, she grabbed a hat, a pair of flat sandals and hurried back down the stairs.

As her feet hit the main level, she heard a voice in the back of her head.

You haven't changed at all. You still run when things get tough.

Rick's words echoed, making her come to a stop.

She didn't, she wanted to protest. There were times to stay and fight and times for a sensible retreat. That's what had happened this afternoon. A sensible retreat. Nothing more. But of course he wouldn't see it that way. He would see it the way he wanted—so that he looked good and she was the bad guy. In fact—

A knock on the front door made her freeze in place. No one she knew should be showing up here. Her father had left for a few weeks in the south of France. Several of her teacher friends were traveling with their families. The others were busy with summer jobs or—

Mandy slapped the hat against her bare thigh. Why was she hesitating? There was only one person who would come calling here. As her car was parked right in front of the house, it was unlikely that he was going away anytime soon.

She sucked in a breath, then walked to the door and pulled it open.

Rick stood there. Like her, he'd changed into shorts and a T-shirt. He was tall, tanned and not smiling. Nor could she see his eyes. Dark glasses hid them from view.

Her heart fluttered, her stomach started that pesky

roller-coaster movement again and a blush flared on her cheeks.

''How did you find me?'' she asked.

He removed his sunglasses, allowing her to see emotions flickering through his blue eyes. Not that she could read any of them.

''I know Cassie's last name. With that information and a general idea of where the house was located, it wasn't difficult.''

She nodded. Rick had always been a whiz on a computer.

She stepped back to allow him in, then closed the door and followed him into the living room. He glanced around. When he motioned to the sofa, she nodded again, taking a seat across from him in an old club chair.

To her mind, Cassie's summer home had always been a wonderful place to visit. A block from the ocean, the sunny patio with the BBQ and comfortable furniture had made this pretty darned close to paradise. Right up until she'd seen Rick's place. By comparison, the beach house was barely an upgraded double-wide.

Perspective, she thought, trying to find the humor in the situation. Life was all about perspective.

''I'm sorry about what happened,'' Rick said, setting his sunglasses on the worn coffee table between them and resting his forearms on his thighs. ''Seeing each other after all these years was enough of a shock without throwing anything else into the mix. I guess the chemistry got the better of us.'' He gave her a slight smile. ''I was never a fan of chemistry.''

''It certainly seems to have gotten us into trouble,'' she said with a shrug. While she appreciated his apology, she wasn't exactly sure what he meant by it. Was he sorry they'd made love? Or for what happened afterward? Not that she was feeling brave enough to ask at the moment.

"I'm sorry, too," she said, and made a vague gesture.

He nodded. "I started thinking after you left. About why my mom suggested we get together. You know she doesn't do anything without a reason. In this case she was right, we *do* have unfinished business between us."

His words were a little too close to what she and Cassie had talked about for comfort. She shifted in her seat. "Is that a surprise? I would think most divorced couples have left a few untrimmed threads. Does that have to be significant?"

He raised his eyebrows. "Mandy, two hours ago we were making love. I'm going to guess that makes our untrimmed threads damned significant."

Well, if he was going to put it like *that*. "Okay. Maybe." She rubbed her temples. Trouble was coming; she could feel it all the way down to her bones.

"I think we need to straighten this out so we can both move on with our lives," he said.

She glared at him. "I've sort of figured that out for myself."

With a little help from Cassie. Not that she wanted to. Let the threads dangle—that was her motto. Except there was every possibility that Rick was the reason she hadn't once fallen in love in the past eight years.

"I thought you might," he said. "So what do we do now?"

She sighed. Lord but she hated being mature. "I

don't know. Spend time together, I guess. Talk about stuff.'' She narrowed her gaze. ''Stay out of bed.''

A flicker of fire flared to life in his eyes. ''You sure about that one?''

''Absolutely.''

She was lying, but he didn't have to know that.

''I'll agree to your terms,'' he said. ''But only on one condition.''

''Which is?''

''You won't tell my mom she was right.''

Mandy stared at him, then burst out laughing. He had a point. Jo would hold it over them for months.

''I won't say a word,'' she promised. ''I don't want to hear about it any more than you do.'' She leaned forward a little. ''This is a real mess. How did we get here?''

''I don't know. You're the woman. Aren't you supposed to be the relationship expert?''

He was being funny, but she didn't smile. ''I'm hardly an expert. If I was…a lot of things would have been different.''

''Like what?''

Like a thousand things, she thought sadly. ''I would have talked to you more. Told you what I was feeling. I wouldn't have—'' Gee, they were going to jump right into this, weren't they? ''I wouldn't have used sex as a weapon.''

He winced. ''We're both guilty of using sex to get what we wanted,'' he said. ''I used it to tell you I cared about you, because saying the words made me feel weak, as if I was giving you the upper hand.''

She hadn't known that, but the information didn't surprise her. ''I used sex to keep you in line and get what I wanted. When I didn't, I withheld. Not my finest hour.'' She rested her elbows on her knees and her chin on her hands. ''I wanted to feel that you were close to me emotionally, but all I could get was the physical.''

''I don't know that I was capable of more. Not then.''

And now? But she didn't ask that. Besides, she already knew the answer.

''More if onlys,'' she said. ''If only we'd been more grown-up. If only we'd talked. If only I hadn't run back to my dad's that last time and—''

She pressed her lips together to hold back the words. Not that there was any point. Rick already knew what had happened.

Embarrassment swept over her. She straightened and fought the urge to change the subject. Except they needed to talk about this—about the fact that Rick had fooled around with some woman but hadn't gone all the way, while she'd slept with a stranger.

''Mandy, we don't have to go there.''

''Why? It was significant.''

''Sure, but the marriage was already pretty much over.''

Amazing. After all this time, he was trying to spare her feelings. She didn't know what that meant. Especially when she'd been the one to cheat.

''I was so angry,'' she said, almost unable to stop herself from telling the truth, maybe for the first time ever. ''After I saw you with that grad student, I was furious. I went to the airport and got on the first plane back to L.A. By the time I got to my dad's it was nine or ten at night. I don't remember. There was a party.'' She swallowed. ''Back then there was always a party.''

She could remember walking into his spacious Beverly Hills mansion. People spilled out of every room. Most of them were drunk, or on their way to being so. By then Mandy had calmed down enough to feel pain, as well as rage. It was as if someone had played handball with her heart. She hated Rick and longed for him in equal measures.

Her father had listened, held her and told her it would be okay. But then he'd been called away and someone had pressed a drink in her hand.

"I hadn't eaten," she said. "I'd spent the whole plane trip crying. The liquor hit me." She shrugged. "That's a pretty pitiful excuse."

She'd been sitting alone in a corner when some up-and-coming young male star had found her. They'd talked for a while. She couldn't remember about what. She could barely remember his name or what he'd looked like.

"He offered and I said yes. Because I wanted to hurt you." She squeezed her eyes shut. "It was horrible. I'd never done anything like that before. Had sex with a stranger. It's not the fun and happy good time it's cracked up to be. You walked in on us the next morning."

Rick's expression turned haunted. Mandy ached for both of them. She could still remember the sun piercing her eyes as she wrestled with a hangover the size of Montana. She'd barely made it to the bathroom before throwing up. When she'd staggered back to her bed, she'd been stunned to find a guy in it.

All the memories of the previous night had crashed in on her. Then, before she could make sense of them, Rick had walked into her room. It had been the only time he hadn't let her go.

No matter how long she lived, she would never forget the look on his face.

"I never said I was sorry," she whispered. "I was, from the very first, and I still am. It was selfish and stupid and incredibly immature."

He shrugged. "I knew why you'd done it. I'd caused you pain for so long."

His excusing her behavior stunned her. "So it didn't matter?"

His eyes darkened. "It mattered."

"Oh, Rick. What a mess."

He nodded. "I couldn't be what you wanted, what you needed."

"I had the same problem," she admitted. "You wanted the perfect social hostess, housekeeper and mistress. I was twenty and didn't know anything about being married."

He straightened. "You know, I've yet to find that perfect combination. I wonder why that is."

"It doesn't exist." She sucked in a breath. Some of the pain inside her eased a little. "Maybe you should try inventing a robot."

"That was my first plan. Instead I've been trying to change my requirements to something more realistic. I think I would be happier with an imperfect flesh-and-blood partner rather than a perfect machine. Besides, I'm hardly Mr. Wonderful."

"You have your moments," she said, even though her chest felt as if a thousand pounds were pressing in on it.

What was wrong with her? She should be happy that Rick had reached the place in his life where he was ready to be in a serious relationship. Didn't she want him to get married again?

She told herself she did, that she wasn't envious of the woman who would be lucky enough to claim him. She, Mandy, had already had her shot and she'd blown it. Besides, it wasn't as if she had feelings for him. Not after all this time.

She cleared her throat. "So what are your current requirements?"

"The usual. A wife. Kids. Maybe a couple of dogs. My work can be difficult. It's generally challenging. I want to have something more to come home to than an empty house. More balance."

"We've been using the 'b' word a lot today," she told him.

"You're right. Has it just been today?" He shook his head. "Feels like a lot longer to me."

To her, too, but it had just been the one day.

"How long until Cassie joins you?" he asked.

"A couple of weeks."

"Until then are you open to spending time together? I'll need to head into the office for a day or so to get things in order. Then I'll take some time off. Maybe we can learn to be friends."

The pressure on her chest eased a little. "I'd like that." She managed a smile. Friends. That was what they should be, she told herself, even as she had a fleeting thought that there was a lot of potential for more.

"We'll work on the past," she said as he rose to his feet. "Figure out this closure thing and get on with our lives."

"Exactly."

She stood and he smiled at her. "How about if I come by day after tomorrow," he said. "About ten in the morning?"

"Sounds good."

Better than good, she thought as he waved and left. Then she stopped herself in mid mental-sentence. No way. She and Rick had a very specific purpose. Apparently they hadn't finished up with each other as much as they should have. If she could tie up all the loose ends with him, she could move on with her life. That's what she wanted. Not a slow walk down memory lane. Been there, done that. It hadn't worked the first time and there was no reason to think it would work this time.

Right?

Oddly enough, there was no answer.

Chapter Six

Mandy stretched out in the chair, her feet resting on the railing around the deck. It was an amazing day—warm, sunny, not a cloud in the sky. She had a perfect view of the ocean, a cold lemonade in her hand. She could get used to life like this.

In the background she could hear Rick's voice. He was arguing with someone, but she refused to pay attention. When he got off the phone, he would tell her all about it…probably with a lot of passion in his voice. In the past few days she had discovered Rick was passionate about a lot of things. His work, the house, his hobbies.

Her?

Don't go there, she told herself. Dangerous, dangerous territory. One fabulous afternoon in bed did not a relationship make. She and Rick were looking for an ending, not a beginning. Still, a girl could dream.

She had discovered he was the kind of man who made dreaming easy. They'd spent much of the past seven days in each other's company. Going to lunch, the movies. They'd taken an all-day sail, had cooked out on the beach, picked out new flooring and fixtures for the guest bath in his house, and had generally hung out. By mutual agreement, they'd avoided any difficult topics, instead using the time to get to know each other.

With Rick, the more she learned, the more she liked. They got along well, agreed on many subjects, disagreed on enough to keep things interesting. There was also the added spice of the chemistry between them.

It lurked in the background, never obvious, but never absent. It was as if everything inside her vibrated slightly when he was near. The sensation was acutely pleasant.

She closed her eyes and did her best to get lost in the moment. Whatever she might feel about Rick was interesting, but not significant. They weren't ever going to be more than what they were. Now if he'd been like this eight years ago, things might have been different.

Her eyes popped open and she sighed. Honesty insisted that she acknowledge that unless she got the chance to go back and make her former self more mature, the marriage was still doomed to failure. She'd had unrealistic expectations about the relationship from the start.

She heard Rick slam down the phone and mutter something. He stalked out to the deck and flopped down in the chair next to hers. She adjusted her sun hat so she could see him and lowered her sunglasses on her nose.

"What's wrong?"

He shrugged and reached for his lemonade. "I'm arguing with the board about a project. It's a pet project of John's—he's on the board. He wants me to approve it, but it doesn't work. We've recreated the experiment three times and the results don't match what the inventor told us they would be. I don't know where he got his data, but it wasn't using this particular experiment. I recommended that we pass on the project."

Mandy shoved her glasses back in place. "Let me guess. John's having a cow about the whole thing."

Some of Rick's tension eased as he grinned. "I wouldn't have phrased it that way, but, yes."

She grinned. "There's nothing like hanging out with a bunch of kids to keep one's descriptions creative."

"I guess."

They were both casually dressed in shorts and shirts. She wasn't sure what he thought of her attire, but she was darned appreciative of his long, powerful legs and the way his shoulders filled out his T-shirt. She took a sip of lemonade to cool herself down and returned her attention to the conversation at hand.

"So what happens now?" she asked.

"We argue." He shrugged. "It's pretty common at the foundation. Everyone is brilliant and everyone has an opinion. Very few projects get through easily. But that's what makes things work. John knew I'd tell him the truth when he asked me to review the material. I don't think he knew the information was bogus. Now he's mad, but he'll get over it.''

"So you won't get in trouble for disagreeing with the boss?"

"Not even close." He set his glass back on the table. "The frustrating part is we've run the experiment three times. John knows that in science, like in life, if you put the same elements together in the same way, you get the same result."

She straightened in her chair. "That doesn't happen in life."

"Sure it does."

"Not if there are people involved. No two situations are ever exactly the same outside of a controlled environment. Life is many things, but it's not controlled."

He didn't look convinced.

"What about us?" she continued. "We're not the same people we were eight years ago. We're completely different, so this situation is completely different."

"If that's true, then the elements aren't the same."

"My point is people aren't elements."

"They can be."

She rolled her eyes. "You're being deliberately difficult."

A smile tugged at the corner of his mouth. "Maybe."

"Figures." She decided a change of subject would be best for both of them. "I'm heading back to Los Angeles for a couple of days. I received a call last night from Daisy, Eva's foster mother. Eva's the little girl I told you about."

"I remember. Is everything all right?"

"Yes. I have official permission to spend time with Eva, so I thought I'd start by going to the Long Beach aquarium with her. Eva really likes the ocean and things that live in it."

"Sounds like fun."

"I hope it will be."

Mandy tried to act casual about the whole thing, but she was pretty excited. Although she still wasn't sure that she would have the guts to adopt a special-needs child on her own, she wanted to seriously consider the possibility. Rather than simply spend time with Eva, she'd gone through the process of receiving official clearance so there would be no holdup if she did go forward with the adoption. Better to be prudent than make waves.

Rick leaned back in his chair. "Want company?"

She stared at him. "What?"

"I'm not doing anything for the next couple of days. We could go down in my car. Spend the night in some fancy hotel." He held up his free hand. "Separate rooms. I know. No fooling around in the name of closure." He shrugged. "I thought it might be fun."

She didn't understand. No man in her acquaintance had ever been willing to get within throwing distance of Eva. "Are you talking about coming to the aquarium with us?" she asked cautiously.

"If you wouldn't mind."

His obvious acceptance of the situation surprised her. But then she reminded herself that they were nothing but friends working on the past.

"Um, that would be great. Thanks."

As there was going to be a young child to worry about, they drove down in Rick's sedan rather than his convertible.

"Safety versus flash," he said as they pulled into the modest Torrance neighborhood. "She doesn't need a car seat or anything, does she?"

Mandy shook her head. "She's eight. She'll be fine in the back seat."

She directed him to turn right at the corner, then left at the stop sign. Although she spoke calmly, he could feel her tension. It filled the car until he wanted to take her twisting fingers in his and promise that it would be all right. However, he didn't think she could believe him.

He could see that this was a big deal for Mandy. Obviously she cared about the kid a lot. He was interested in meeting Eva and seeing how the afternoon went. No one had defined the term "special needs" so he didn't know what more Eva might need as compared with a child who wasn't categorized that way.

While Rick would never admit it to Mandy, he wasn't keen on labeling kids. He'd been badged as "gifted" before he was five. The word—both a blessing and a curse—had followed him right into high school, which he'd entered at eleven. He'd entered college at thirteen. It had taken him the full four years to graduate because he'd double majored in computer science and physics. He'd finished his first master's and Ph.D. by the time he was twenty and was on to his second when he'd met Mandy. He knew all about being different.

He pulled up in front of the one-story house by the corner. Mandy was out of the car before he'd done much more than put it in park. She hovered by the passenger door. As he watched, a child flew out of the front door of the house and raced down the walk. Rick had a brief impression of long blond hair, a wide, happy smile and open arms before the two flung themselves at each other.

"How are you?" Mandy was asking as he climbed out of the car. "Are you having a good summer? I've missed you."

"I missed you. We've had fun. Daisy took us to the pool twice and we saw fireworks on the Fourth of July and—"

Eva's happy chatter came to a halt as Rick circled around the rear of the car. She gave him a quick glance then ducked behind Mandy.

"Eva, don't be scared. This is Rick."

Before she could say more, a cheerful but harried-looking woman in her thirties came out the front door. "Mandy," she called with a smile. "Someone has been parked by the front window for the past hour, hasn't she?"

Eva ducked her head out from behind Mandy, grinned, then retreated.

"Daisy!" Mandy gave the other woman a warm hug. "How are you doing?"

Daisy shook her head. "Going crazy. I got a call this morning asking if I could provide emergency shelter for toddler twins. Just what I need. Of course I said yes." She turned to Rick. "Hi. I'm Daisy Middleton."

"Rick Benson."

"He's an old friend," Mandy said quickly, as if concerned he was going to come up with another title.

"Old friend works," he said with a quick wink.

Daisy looked intrigued but didn't ask any questions. Instead she rested one hand on Eva's blond head and the other on Mandy's arm. "There was some other news in the phone call," she said pointedly. "I'm not supposed to say anything, so act surprised when you get the news."

She paused significantly until Mandy chuckled. "Don't keep me in suspense. What news?"

"You were approved for foster care. They start you with one child, but that's all you want, isn't it?"

Mandy didn't say anything. Her eyes widened and she looked stunned. Rick glanced between the women, looking for an explanation.

Just then three more young children spilled out of the house. Daisy saw them and groaned. "No. You were supposed to be napping." She started toward them, then turned back. "Run for it while you can. Oh, we're having a cookout with the neighbors, so can you have her back by four-thirty?"

"No problem," Mandy called after her.

She ushered Eva into the car and settled her in the middle of the big back seat. Once everyone had on their seat belts, Rick started the car and headed back toward the freeway. Mandy fiddled with the radio.

"There's a kid's station, if you don't mind," she said.

"Not at all. I can even do you one better." He pushed a button, sending the sound into the rear speakers. "Instant child-friendly sound."

"Thanks." She glanced over her shoulder. "Are you okay, Eva?"

"Uh-huh."

Mandy smiled. "Are you going to still be shy around Rick when we get to the aquarium?"

A pause, then, "Uh-huh."

Both he and Mandy laughed. "I'll try bribing her

with ice cream when we get there,'' he said. ''It always worked with me.''

''I'll have to remember that.''

He shot her a quick look. ''You okay?''

''Nervous.''

He lowered his voice. ''What did Daisy mean back there when she said you'd been approved for foster care?''

Mandy leaned toward him and spoke softly. In the back seat Eva was singing along with a song about happy frogs.

''I've been approved to be a foster parent. That's the first step in anything permanent. Eva would come stay with me as a foster child and we would see how things go.'' She leaned back in her seat. ''Now I have to get real about this. It's no longer in the abstract.''

''Scary?''

She looked at him and nodded. ''More than you know. I want to do the right thing for both of us. I worry about having the right resources.''

''You wouldn't have to worry about money. Your dad would see to that.''

''I'm all grown up. Isn't it time to stop expecting him to bail me out?''

''This is different.''

''Maybe. There are other considerations. It's a huge, lifetime commitment. I want to do things right. I want to be sure. Actually, I want us both to be sure.''

Rick glanced in his rearview mirror. Eva beamed as she sang. Every couple of seconds she looked at Mandy. Her whole face lit up with delight. Mandy might need to be sure, but it seemed that Eva had already made up her mind.

"I can see the responsibility would be a little daunting," he said.

"That's part of it."

He tried to imagine what he would do in her situation. Mandy's affection for Eva came from knowing the child. He didn't have much contact with kids. He frowned. Actually he didn't have any.

The thought came from nowhere that if he and Mandy had stayed together, they would have several children by now. Well, at least a couple.

What would that have been like? He wanted to think that they would have been good parents, but he wasn't sure. They'd both needed to grow up. Things would be different now. Not that they were talking about kids, or anything but getting closure on their divorce.

He looked at Eva again. She caught his gaze in the mirror and gave him a shy smile. He smiled back. Next to him Mandy hummed along with the song. Her nerves had faded and she seemed happy, as well. All in all, it was turning out to be a good day.

"Look!" Rick said, pointing overhead.

Eva obligingly craned her neck, then gasped, took a step back and nearly toppled over. Rick caught her with a steadying hand on her waist.

"It's a whale," he said. "A blue whale. They're the biggest creatures on the planet."

Eva looked from the full-scale model to him and back. "Where?" she asked.

"In the water."

She glanced at the aquarium tanks around them and looked doubtful.

"Not here," he said. "Out in the ocean. There's a chart over there. I'll show you."

He held out his hand and Eva took it with a trust that brought a lump to Mandy's throat. Somehow on the short walk from the car to the entrance to the Aquarium of the Pacific, Rick had managed to charm the shy eight-year-old. Now he led her to the display that detailed where blue whales lived.

Two hours later, Mandy found herself as charmed as Eva. They'd toured the first level of the display before moving upstairs to the second level. Over snacks in the Café Scuba, Rick kept them both laughing with stories about his various scuba-diving adventures.

"You swim under the water?" Eva asked, obviously impressed by such an impossible feat.

"With help," he said. "Can you swim?"

Eva sipped on her covered cup of milk and shrugged. "Daisy takes us to the pool, but I don't swim. I have water wings," she added. "Sometimes I kick my feet."

Mandy bit her tongue. She wanted to say something about lessons and Eva learning, but she didn't. She didn't want to get the girl's hopes up.

Around them other families ate and talked together. She caught the occasional stare aimed their way. One little boy of four or five had loudly asked what was wrong with Eva. Before Mandy could do anything, Rick had stepped between Eva and the family, pointing out a display of brightly colored fish.

Down syndrome children were often the object of stares. Mandy understood why, but that didn't make her like it. Still, far from being upset or uncomfortable, Rick had simply gone with the flow. She appreciated that. She turned her attention back to the conversation at hand.

"Daddies have the babies?" Eva asked, sounding doubtful.

Rick read from the brochure he'd picked up by one of the displays. "Apparently that's common with all sea horses. Here at the aquarium there have been successful transfers of eggs—"

He broke off and saw Eva's blank expression. He laughed and touched the tip of her nose. "Sorry. Yes. Daddies have the babies." He scanned the paper. "They carry the eggs on the underside of their tails." He looked at Mandy and winked. "Sounds a bit fishy to me."

She chuckled. "I don't know. I think most women like the idea of the male of the species being more involved with the birth process." She turned to Eva. "Mommies like daddies to help."

Eva nodded. "Daisy tells Frank to get off his butt sometimes. He kisses her when he thinks we're not looking."

"Good for him," Rick said. "Ready for the sea lions and seals again?" he asked.

"Yes, yes!"

Eva jumped to her feet. Her milk went flying. Rick caught the container easily and dumped it into a trash can without saying a word.

Mandy followed them. They'd already spent time watching the aquatic mammals in their exhibit, but Eva wanted to see them again. Rick didn't seem to mind the repeat viewing. He even held Eva high in his arms to give her a bird's-eye view.

This was how it would be if she found someone, Mandy thought, feeling both happy and unsettled.

This was what she wanted for Eva and for herself. A family. But if that wasn't possible…

She didn't have an answer for that. Not yet. She loved Eva, but the responsibility terrified her. What if she didn't do it right? What if she messed up Eva forever? Having someone else around would give her support, a sounding board and another opinion of how things were going. Plus Eva deserved all the love she could get.

As in many other aspects of life, there weren't any easy answers.

They finished their outing with a stop at the gift shop. Rick insisted on buying them each a stuffed animal. He also bought Eva a brightly colored book about the various creatures at the aquarium, then adopted a weedy sea dragon in her name.

"Why are you being so nice?" she asked as they walked back to the car.

"I'm not. I'm having a good time. Aren't you?"

She nodded.

Eva stumbled over a crack in the pavement. Mandy reached for her, but Rick got there first. He caught the child up in his arms and carried her toward the car.

"No skinned knees today," he said lightly as they went. "I remember them and boy do they hurt bad."

"You could kiss it, make it better."

"Yes, I could. But maybe it would be nice if you didn't get a skinned knee at all."

"Okay," Eva said. She glanced over his shoulder and beamed at Mandy. "I had fun today."

"Me, too."

It had been a revelation. All week she'd been fighting against her physical attraction to Rick. The more time they spent together, the more she found to like about him. But something else had happened today. Something far more dangerous than simply sexual attraction.

Today she'd seen a side of him that she didn't know existed. He'd been patient, kind and completely accepting. What made the combination even more devastating was that she knew he'd done it without conscious thought. He'd simply been himself. In his mind, they'd taken Eva out for the day, so the best of all possible scenarios was that everyone have a good time. It had been as simple as that.

Only it wasn't simple for her. Not when her insides felt exposed and raw. He could seduce her body with just a look, but it took a lot more to seduce her heart. Somehow he'd made both happen today, which meant she was in more trouble than she'd first thought.

Chapter Seven

The beachfront restaurant had a small dance floor that extended out over the sand. A three-piece combo offered quiet accompaniment to the dinner conversation, while a few brave couples took a turn around the floor.

Mandy swirled the wine in her glass, watching the ruby-colored liquid catch and release light. She and Rick had returned Eva to Daisy, then they'd driven to the hotel and checked in. The separate bedrooms he'd promised turned out to be part of the same suite, but she hadn't protested. In her current state—with her mind confused and tipping and unable to grasp even the most basic of concepts—protesting about rooms was completely beyond her.

She didn't know what to do—about Rick, about Eva, about her life. Three weeks ago everything had been so clear. She had plans for the future and definite ideas about the past. Now all that had changed, leaving her out of sorts.

"What are you thinking about?" Rick asked.

She shrugged rather than answer. She couldn't tell him *everything* that was on her mind. At least not the part about him. As to the rest of it...

"Eva mostly. Today was great."

"I thought so."

She leaned toward him, taking in the dark hair, the deep blue eyes, the easy smile. "You were wonderful with her." She held up a hand before he could speak. "I know you weren't trying especially hard or doing anything out of the ordinary. That's what makes it so special."

He frowned. "I'm not sure I know what you're talking about, but thanks, anyway."

"You're welcome." She sighed. "Eva had a good time, too, which is what I wanted. I don't think I've ever seen her so happy and comfortable. Usually she takes time to warm up to strangers, but not today."

"Then why are you sad?"

"I'm not sad, exactly. More wistful."

"That's a subtlety you'll have to explain."

She gave him a quick smile. "Fair enough. I've been thinking about Eva and whether or not I have what it takes to adopt her. I work with children like her all the time, but that's very different from being responsible for them. I've never had a child. What if I do everything wrong? What if I make her life worse?"

He reached across their small table and touched her hand. "Sometimes you have to lead with your heart."

"You think?"

"I'm sure of it. What every child needs is to be

loved unconditionally. To know his or her world is safe. To have the freedom to grow and learn and be. Everything else is gravy.''

Mandy stared at him in surprise. ''For someone who talks about people in terms of experiments and elements, that's pretty insightful.''

''I'm a deep kind of guy.'' He squeezed her fingers, then released her hand. ''Seriously, I've learned a thing or two in the past few years, and one of them is that once the heart is involved, there are plenty of things that can't be explained. Every now and then, we all have to take it on faith. That includes loving and being loved.''

He smiled. ''Eva's a special little girl. I can see why you want to adopt her. She cries out for a family of her own, which is what you always wanted. You couldn't give it to yourself, but you *can* give it to her. Does rewriting the past make the situation more appealing to you? Probably. Does that matter? I doubt it.''

Mandy stared at him openmouthed. She couldn't believe it. In five seconds, with a few simple sentences, Rick had just explained her relationship with Eva and clarified her—until now—undefined feelings of longings.

She *had* always longed for a family of her own. Her father loved her very much, but he was usually running off to make a movie somewhere. She'd grown up mostly alone. When it had become clear that her father wasn't going to remarry and provide her with the home and family she'd always wanted, she made friends with girls who had families in place, then got involved with them.

Now, all these years later, was she really trying to

make up for that by giving Eva a family? It made sense. And as Rick had said—it didn't much matter. As long as she was willing to make the commitment to take on this child.

"Ten points for your team," she said slowly. "Like I said. Insightful."

"I've come to know you in the past couple of weeks," he told her. "Which is funny, because I would have said I knew you before." He shook his head. "I didn't at all. I see that now. I saw what I wanted to see. Now I can see the real you."

"There's a scary thought." She sipped her wine. "I'll agree with you. I didn't know you all that well before, either. Actually I didn't get men at all. It took me a while to realize that I wasn't looking for a flesh-and-blood male to share my life. Instead I wanted some handsome prince from a fairy story to rescue me from my life and sweep me away. I wanted to be the princess—worshiped rather than loved."

"Your own personal pedestal?" he asked, his voice low and teasing.

"Something like that. I even found a few guys interested in the same fantasy."

"What happened?"

"Life on a pedestal isn't all it's cracked up to be. When a man treats a woman like a princess, there isn't much room left for real life. There certainly isn't any room for a child like Eva. I found out I was much happier on solid ground."

"Sounds like a good lesson. Similar to what I learned about wanting a real flesh-and-blood woman and not some perfect robot."

"*Perfect.* There's that word again. Why is it so hard to give up?" she asked.

"I'm not sure. Because it's not real? Maybe we all chase illusions. Maybe they're safer."

Mandy didn't know how to respond to that. Before she could figure out an answer, Rick rose and held out his hand.

"Dance with me?"

They were both still casually dressed from their day at the aquarium. Their dinner would be arriving any second and the dance floor was small and exposed. Still Mandy stood and placed her hand on his, allowing him to lead her to the edge of the restaurant. When he turned toward her, she slipped easily into his arms.

The sun had set an hour or so before, and the moon rose behind them. She could see the first fingers of moonlight drifting across the ocean. Then Rick pulled her close and it was so much easier to close her eyes and let the world drift away.

They swayed together to the gentle rhythm of the music. Nothing else mattered but being close. His heat surrounded her, as did his scent. Her skin began to tingle as her heart rate increased. Desire swept through her. Over the past couple of weeks, she'd managed to keep her attraction to him at bay, but it suddenly burst free, threatening to overwhelm her.

She became conscious of their skin touching—bare legs brushing as they swayed together, his fingers laced with hers. Every movement, every breath became an erotic counterpoint to their slow dancing. Her breasts swelled. Between her legs, wanting grew.

What was wrong with her? Why was she reacting like this? Why now? The urge to run was strong, but the need to stay in his embrace was stronger still.

She was so caught up in trying to stay in control

she barely noticed when they stopped moving. Rick cupped her face in his hands and stared into her eyes.

"I know we're not supposed to do much more than find closure. I agree that your plan is sensible. The hell of it is, I want you more than I want my next breath. Touching you like this…being with you. I'm on fire, Mandy. I figured I'd better just tell you, because I don't think I can stand sharing that suite with you tonight. Not without coming on to you, which I know you don't want. I guess my point is we need to drive back to Santa Barbara after dinner."

His words nearly blew her away. She saw desire tightening the features of his face. Tension hardened every part of his body and she didn't doubt that if she swayed a little closer, she would find physical proof of his arousal.

Yes, she'd come up with the rules and they were really sensible. Only a fool would risk taking things to the next level, just when they were—in theory— trying to finish with each other.

Wasn't sensible highly overrated?

She leaned close and brushed his mouth with hers.

"I'm not really hungry," she said. "Are you?"

He didn't speak. Instead he stared at her as if unable to believe what she was saying.

"So maybe we should just go upstairs," she continued.

"And pack?"

"No. And stay."

His pupils dilated. "Mandy, are you sure?"

"Not really, but I know that I want you. As you seem to want me…" She cleared her throat. "I could go the 'we're both sensible adults route' but the truth is this is crazy. I'll admit it. I'm guessing you will, too. Let's be crazy together.''

He grabbed her hand in a death grip and pulled her toward the table just as the waiter appeared with their entrées.

''Something's come up,'' Rick said, then grinned at his own pun. ''Charge dinner to the room.'' He gave the waiter their room number, then tugged her toward the exit, calling back, ''Don't forget to tip yourself.''

Then they were in the elevator. Even before the doors closed, Rick pulled her close and began kissing her. She felt the pressure of his mouth on hers, the heat of him. He licked her bottom lip, then when she opened to admit him, he plunged inside.

He tasted of wine and desire. She wound her arms around his neck and pressed against him, desperate to be as close as possible. Her hips arched forward, bringing her belly in contact with his hard arousal. At the first second of contact, her knees went weak. She dropped a hand to his rear and, before she could stop herself, she drew him even closer and ground herself against him.

His breath caught, then he broke the kiss and swore softly.

''I'm about five seconds from losing control,'' he confessed. ''How do you do that to me?''

''I'm not doing anything.''

He moved both his hands to her rear and pulled her tight. Then he rotated his hips, grinding himself against her.

''You do everything,'' he said with a groan.

She was having a little trouble in the breathing department herself. Plus she needed him to touch her.

This "clothes on" stuff wasn't working at all. Without thinking, she reached for his shirt, only to have the elevator doors open.

Mandy nearly fainted. For the length of their journey to the sixth floor, she'd completely forgotten where she was. That had never happened to her before.

He grabbed her hand and pulled her toward the door to their suite. She was relieved to see that the corridors were deserted. No one had witnessed her wanton behavior.

It wasn't that she regretted her feelings, or her passion, but some things were better done in private.

With some muttering and cursing, he pulled the card key out of his back pocket, then managed to get the door open. They hurried into the spacious living room. Rick slammed the door shut behind them a nanosecond before they fell on each other.

Mandy tugged at his shirt, while he did the same with hers. Unfortunately they couldn't both be pulling T-shirts off each other, so they were forced to break apart, tug off their shirts, then reunite in the center of the room.

"I want you," he breathed, kissing her jaw, then moving to her neck, where he nibbled on the sensitive skin just below her ear. "I want all of you. I've been thinking about this, dreaming about making love with you. I've been reliving that amazing afternoon we spent together in my bed. I knew you were right to say we shouldn't do it again, but that didn't stop me from wanting you."

His words were verbal seduction of the most powerful kind. Mandy felt herself melting inside as she gave herself up to the images he painted. She wanted to tell him she had wanted him, too, that there were nights when sexual flashbacks had kept her from sleeping, but as he was kissing her on the mouth, she found it tough to speak.

Then she didn't want to speak because he'd unfastened her bra and pushed the straps down her arms. As the lingerie fell to the floor, he cupped her breasts in his hands. While he used his fingers to explore her curves, he teased her tight nipples with his thumbs.

Fire shot through her. She clamped her mouth around his tongue and sucked until he moaned. She ran one hand through his hair and dropped the other to his hip. From there it was a short journey around between them to the ridge of need pressing against his fly.

She rubbed the length of him with her palm. He responded by biting her lower lip and moving faster against her nipples. He dropped one hand to her hip, then slid it around. She caught her breath in anticipation, then gasped as he gently squeezed her between her legs.

It was too good, she thought frantically. It wasn't enough. Naked. They had to be naked. Now!

She reached for the fastening of his shorts, but fumbled. He released her, then pushed her hand away and went to work on the button. She did the same on her shorts. Seconds later they were both naked.

He broke the kiss and stared into her face. She didn't know what he saw there, but if the wanting was anything like that which she saw on his face, it was pretty powerful. He lowered one hand and stroked her fanny, tracing the full curve then squeezing slightly. Suddenly he closed his eyes and groaned.

"I hope to hell I've got a condom in my shaving kit."

She stared at him. She could feel her eyes widening and her mouth parting. "I never thought of that." Of course they needed protection. She wasn't on any kind of birth control, and there were other considerations.

Rick took off for the bathroom of the bedroom he was supposed to be using. She watched him go, admiring the movement of powerful muscles, then followed when he disappeared. There was a rustling sound from the bathroom.

"We can do other stuff if we have to," she called.

"I know that, but I really want to be inside of you. I love how hot and wet you feel. It drives me crazy."

His matter-of-fact statement nearly sent her to her knees.

"Got it!"

He came out waving a wrapped condom. Before she could move to the bed, he swooped down and gathered her in his arms.

"I want you," he breathed, kissing her cheeks, her mouth, her jaw. "All of you."

He kissed her neck, then moved lower to her breasts, all the while moving her backward toward the bed. When she came to a stop against the mattress, he tenderly lowered her down, following so that he knelt between her legs. He tossed the protection onto the nightstand and bent low to lick her nipples.

She found herself in the glorious position of simply receiving pleasure. His tender mouth sucked and tugged until she arched off the bed and begged him to let her find her release. Tension spiraled through her, growing and growing. Heat burned between her legs, then began to seep into every part of her body.

Then he moved lower. Lower and lower, kissing his way down her rib cage, across her belly, and lower still. Her legs fell open. He ran his hands down her forearms until their fingers entwined, then he drew them to the apex of her thighs and had her hold herself open for him.

For a long time he did nothing. She risked a quick glance and saw him looking at her...*there*. He glanced up and smiled.

"You're pretty. I like how you look."

Then, with their gazes still locked together, he lightly licked that single point of pleasure. The combination of seeing and feeling nearly made her fly off the bed. She sucked in a breath and surrendered herself to his ministrations.

The man knew what he was doing. He moved slowly at first, varying speed and pressure until he'd figured out what made her beg. Then he concentrated on keeping her begging until he pushed her to the point of frenzied need. Every time she thought she couldn't possibly be pushed any higher, he did just that. Higher and more, licking, sucking, nibbling, creating magic.

He slipped a finger inside of her, mimicking the act of lovemaking to follow. The combination nearly made her scream. She tossed her head from side to side as she lost herself in the growing, uncontrollable need to...to...

And then he pushed her over the edge. Her orgasm crashed through her, an endless wave of glorious surrender. She melted into a white-hot puddle, reassembled, then melted again. When the world stopped spinning, she found herself lying in his arms, staring up at his eyes, watching him smile down at her.

"I'm boneless," she whispered. "Completely boneless. I'll never be able to walk again."

"Then we'll just have to lie here, making love forever."

That sounded like a good plan to her. Right up until something very impressive nudged her thigh. She reached down and encircled him.

The second her fingers touched his velvet-over-steel arousal, something flickered back to life within her. She wouldn't have thought it was physically possible for her to become interested again so quickly, but the ache returned and she longed to have him bury himself inside.

"You haven't lost the condom, have you?" she teased.

He grinned. "Not even for a second."

While he rolled on the protection, she rose to her knees. When he was finished, she settled herself over him and slowly sank onto him. He filled her completely…deliciously. It was too amazing, she thought, losing herself in the sensation.

He didn't help when he slipped a hand between her thighs and brushed his thumb against her still-throbbing center. A half dozen or so strokes later and she felt herself soaring again. She rose and fell, caressing him, filling herself. He settled his free hand on her hip to guide her to the right rhythm.

She wanted to watch. She wanted to see the passion overtake him, but as her own need grew, her eyelids fluttered closed. There was only the feel of the man inside her and the way he continued to touch her between her legs.

Tension grew. She felt it in him, as well. Faster and faster she rode him until the end was in sight, then inevitable. Her body convulsed in release, clamping around him, daring him not to give way, as well.

He stiffened, then called out her name. She felt him shudder, and she shuddered herself. Then she braced her arms on the bed and bent toward him. He wrapped his arms around her, pulling her close, settling her on his chest and brushing her hair out of her face.

Their hearts still thundered, in unison, she noticed as the world returned to focus. The steady beating slowed slightly. Her body ached in the best way possible. Tiny aftershocks rippled through her.

"Even better than that first time," she whispered.

"I'll agree. My theory is all that mental practice. I've been imagining this for nearly two weeks."

She smiled weakly, wondering if she had the same excuse. While she had been thinking about making love with Rick, she hadn't been as specific. For her it had been more vague and slightly romantic. Moonlight, flowers, declarations of—

She pushed herself off his chest and stared at him.

"What?" he asked.

"Nothing."

Nothing that she could share with him. Not without them both thinking she was crazy.

She slid off him and slipped under the covers while he disappeared into the bathroom. When he reappeared, she forced herself to smile and act normal. As normal as was possible under the circumstances.

"I thought we might lie here until we get enough strength to shrug into the bathrobes hanging in the bathroom. Then we can call room service and order the dinner we just missed.''

''Sounds like a plan,'' she said, pleased that her voice didn't seem to be giving anything away.

He put an arm around her and drew her next to him. ''I'd like to spend the night with you,'' he said. ''We don't have to make love if you don't want to, but I would like you close.''

She rested her cheek on his shoulder. ''I'd like that, too. Both the sleeping and the making love.''

''Really?''

She smiled. ''Yeah.''

There was no point in *not* making love with him, she told herself as she breathed in the scent of his body and felt her heart constrict a little. Somewhere along the way she'd fallen in love with Rick. Or worse, she'd never stopped loving him. Whichever it was didn't matter. Either way, she was a goner.

Chapter Eight

"You all right?" Rick asked, giving Mandy a quick look as they drove north from Los Angeles.

"Sure." She smoothed the hem of her shorts and smiled. "Why wouldn't I be?"

There was a question he couldn't answer. If he could, he probably wouldn't be wondering about it in the first place.

Something was different. *She* was different. He couldn't figure out what it was, but he sensed it with a certainty that made the hairs at the back of his neck stand up.

The feeling had first come over him sometime in the night. He'd awakened to find Mandy on her side, awake and watching him. When he'd asked her what was wrong, she hadn't answered. Instead she'd slid close and started making love with an intensity that had left him shuddering and out of breath.

They'd made love before and the experience had been extraordinary. He tried to tell himself that what had happened to them in the middle of the night was no different, but he didn't believe the words. It *had* been different and he couldn't say why.

Then, this morning, Mandy hadn't been herself. She'd been friendly enough, and affectionate. Their shower together was proof of that. But there had been something in her eyes. Something that had made him wonder if she was having second thoughts about being with him.

He didn't want to think that, mostly because they were so good together. Yesterday had been proof of that.

Beside him she gave a sigh. "I'm sorry, Rick," she said. "I have a lot on my mind. Cassie should be arriving in a day or so. While I'm really looking forward to hanging out with her, it's going to change things with you and me. We won't be spending as much time together. Which is probably a good thing. I mean you have work and all, right?"

He nodded because he didn't know what to say. He thought about explaining that while he loved his job, it wasn't his world. At least not by choice. He'd always planned that, when he finally met someone and got married again, he would back off on the hours, maybe work something closer to a nine-to-five schedule.

She turned and looked out the window. While Rick believed what she said, he sensed there was more. But what could it be? He thought about the previous day—the time they'd spent with Eva. Thinking about the little girl made him smile. With her big eyes and generous smile, she was something of a charmer.

He'd enjoyed his day with her. A few hours in her presence had clarified Mandy's desire to adopt the little girl. It didn't take much of an imagination to see himself with her. There would be—

He mentally put on the brakes, then backed up big time. *See himself with her?* Was he crazy? Mandy was the one looking to adopt Eva, not him. Sure he'd had a good time with the kid, but that wasn't the same as taking on a lifetime of commitment. Unlike Mandy, he couldn't see himself as a single parent. But with a wife…with someone who shared his dreams, his goals, his heart. Someone like Mandy.

Instead of the freeway, he suddenly saw himself with Eva *and* with Mandy. He saw other children, too. A future, a family.

The clarity and details stunned him, as did the tightness in his chest and the sense of longing.

What the hell was wrong with him? He couldn't possibly have feelings for Mandy. Not now. Not after all this time. No way. Been there, done that. There was no point in taking that road again. He absolutely refused to be falling for her.

He blinked and the vision disappeared. Rather than risk it returning, he concentrated on his driving. At the turnoff for Carpinteria, he turned left without asking if she wanted to go home just yet. *He* needed some time alone to think.

When he reached the beach house, he parked in front. Mandy turned to him.

"I had a really good time," she said, an odd light in her eyes. "I appreciate your help yesterday."

His throat felt scratchy and it was difficult to speak. "I enjoyed it, as well. I'm glad things went well with Eva."

There was an awkward pause, something he didn't expect with Mandy. They were supposed to get along perfectly. Hadn't they always? In the past couple of weeks, words hadn't been their problem.

She shrugged, then reached into the back seat for her small overnight bag. "I guess I'll see you later."

"Sure."

There was so much more he wanted to say. Or was there? Nothing made sense. He wanted…

He didn't know what he wanted, so he let her go. She walked up to the duplex, turned and waved, then disappeared inside. He put the car in gear and headed back to the freeway.

But as he drove, he had the strong sense of just having lost something important. No. That wasn't right. He hadn't lost anything. He and Mandy would still see each other from time to time. The point of this exercise had been to get to know each other again and find closure. They were divorced and had been for years. Why was he rocking the boat now?

He didn't have that answer, or any others. Telling himself that if they tried again, they would only get the same result didn't help. Mandy had insisted that people changed. That *they* had changed. The results wouldn't be the same. He almost believed her.

Then, as he headed north to Santa Barbara, he reached the core of the dilemma. If they were different, were they different enough? Could he trust her not to run? Could she trust him to stay emotionally connected? Had they learned what they needed to in order to make things work a second time around?

The questions stunned him. For the first time in eight years, he didn't know where he stood with Mandy. He felt confused and cautious, yet sure.

In the past eight years, there hadn't been one other woman to come close to capturing his heart. He'd dated them, slept with them, traveled with them, all the while staying emotionally unengaged. He'd thought there might be something wrong with him. Was it that, or was it something else?

Had he found it impossible to fall for anyone else because he'd still been in love with Mandy all this time?

No, he told himself. That wasn't right. He hadn't been waiting for her. He couldn't have been.

As he drove toward the house, he couldn't help wondering how this all was going to end. The chain of events his mother had put in motion with an innocent or not-so-innocent suggestion was turning out to be a hell of a ride.

"I can't believe it, either," Cassie said, sounding frustrated. "I want to get out of here, but it looks like I'm stuck for another five or six days. I'm really sorry."

Mandy clutched the receiver and tried to ignore her rising panic. She'd been desperate for her friend to arrive. Not only did she want to see Cassie, but she'd been hoping for a lot of good advice and a distraction. As it was, she spent all her time thinking about Rick and wondering what she was supposed to do now.

"It must be nice to know they're going to be lost without you," Mandy said.

"Yeah. I'm good at my job. If only my personal life wasn't in the toilet." She gave a sigh. "Oh, well. I suppose I can try to convince myself that things will soon be on an upswing, right?"

"Absolutely. In the meantime, I'll work on my tan and make you jealous."

Cassie laughed. "You use sunscreen with an SPF of about a hundred. How much tan do you think you're going to get?"

Mandy grinned. "It's the thought that counts." Her smile faded. "I miss you."

"I miss you, too. With a little luck, I'll be there in a week." There was a muffled noise in the background. "I have to run. I'll call you later."

"Sure. Okay. Bye."

After hanging up, Mandy paced the length of the living room, then moved outside. But no matter how far she walked, her problems didn't seem to get left behind. They dutifully followed her from place to place, which meant she was going to have to deal with them. Sooner rather than later.

Like maybe now.

She sank into a chair on the patio and closed her eyes. She loved Rick. Her assessment of the problem hadn't changed. She loved him, she might have always loved him. So now what? Did she tell him the truth, like a mature adult, or did she run for the hills?

Her preference was to lace up her athletic shoes, but she knew that wasn't the right thing to do. Running would only make it worse in the long run.

The problem was, she doubted he cared about her the same way. Oh, sure, the sex had been fabulous and they'd had a lot of fun together, but that didn't mean anything. Not to a guy who believed that people were little more than elements of an experiment.

Still, *his* belief system didn't change *her* reality.

She rose and walked back into the house. After sucking in a breath for courage, she picked up the phone and dialed his number from memory. She half expected him to have gone into the office, but he picked up on the first ring.

"Hello?"

"It's me," she said softly, her insides quaking. Great. If it was this bad from several miles away, what was going to happen when they were actually in the same room together? She found she didn't want to think about it.

"What's up?"

"I thought…" She cleared her throat. "I need to talk to you."

"I need to talk to you, too."

"Okay. I thought I'd come over. Is that all right?"

"I'll be waiting."

He *was* waiting, Mandy thought thirty minutes later when she pulled into his driveway. Standing in front of his beautiful house, he watched her park. She didn't allow herself the brief fantasy of what it would be like to live here. Geography was the least of her problems.

She climbed out of the car and crossed to the brick path. Even from here she could see that Rick looked as tense as she felt. Not a good thing, she told herself.

She'd left her purse in the car, so she shoved her car keys into her shorts pocket, then motioned to the house.

"Want to go inside?" she asked.

"Sure."

He let her lead the way.

She came to a stop in the center of the massive foyer. After a second she thought about moving to the living room, but figured she was too nervous to sit just now. Instead she folded her arms over her chest and faced him.

He looked serious. No humor glinted in his eyes; his mouth was pulled in a straight line.

Perfect, she thought grimly. This was so not how she wanted to declare her feelings. She sucked in a breath.

"I'd like to go first, if that's okay."

He nodded. Nothing in his expression gave away his thoughts. Her stomach flopped over.

"So," she said, her voice sounding strained. "The past couple of weeks have showed me that we have more than unfinished business between us. At least that's true for me." She dropped her arms to her sides, then slid her hands into her back pockets.

"We talked about wanting closure. At first I believed that was possible, but now I don't. Mostly because—" she shifted her weight "—I don't think closure happens when one of the parties is still in love with the other." No, that wasn't right.

"Maybe not *still* in love," she amended. "Maybe back in love again. Or still. I don't know."

Nothing. He didn't say a word and he didn't get any more readable. She sighed.

"Okay. So here it is. I'm in love with you. I don't know how much has always been there and how much is new. I just know that's how I feel."

She pressed her lips together and waited. Rick didn't budge. He continued to watch her, without saying a word. Her stomach flopped again, then twisted into a knot. Somehow she'd had the fantasy that he would want to sweep her up in his arms, declare that his feelings were the same, and that they would live happily ever after. Or some variation on that theme.

"It sounds really great," he said at last. "But what happens when things get tough? How long is it going to take you to run away again?"

Ouch. That one hurt. "I'm not like that anymore," she said. "I've changed. Just like you're not the same person you were eight years ago."

"How do I know that? How do I know you won't take off at the first sign of trouble?"

She told herself that the fact he was worried about it was a good thing. It wasn't as if he'd told her he wasn't interested and then had showed her the door. Right?

"You'll have to trust me for now, then see what happens when things get difficult."

"That's not good enough," he told her.

She glared at him. "Oh, right. Because you want a sure thing. So while we're talking about people changing, what about you? You're willing to take plenty of risks in your work, but not in your personal life. You want everything to be a certain way. You want to know the outcome in advance. Well, guess what? This is life, not some laboratory experiment. You don't get a sure thing and you don't get to know the outcome in advance. You have to take a few things on faith. Waiting for the sure thing is only an excuse not to try."

He didn't respond. Her words seemed to echo in the two-story entrance. They reverberated, then crashed back in on Mandy.

She felt as if a lightbulb had just gone off inside her head. Of course. She was guilty of what she'd accused Rick of doing. She'd been using the excuse of not being sure she would get it right to keep herself from trying. The point *wasn't* to get it right, the point was to give a hundred percent. To love fully, to take risks and do the best she could.

That's what had been going on with Eva. Of course she wasn't going to get it right all the time. No one would. But she could love her and be there for her, offering her a stable home and a secure environment.

A calm settled over her as she realized she'd finally gotten it right.

"Life isn't an experiment," she told Rick. "You won't be able to predict the outcome on this one. You have to be willing to risk it. I understand that's scary. Especially with me. We've already failed once. But wouldn't it be amazing if we made it this time?"

He didn't answer. Which was an answer in itself. Maybe he loved her, maybe he didn't. Either way, he wasn't willing to put his feelings on the line.

She turned to leave.

"Already running away?" he taunted.

She shifted until she was looking at him again. "No. I'm running *to* something. I'm driving down to L.A. and filling out the paperwork so that I can become Eva's foster mother. Then I'm going to start the adoption proceedings. Then I'll bring her back to the beach house and we'll start our new life together. I still love you and want us to be together. But I can't make you pick me."

Her heart ached as she looked at him. Letting him go again would be the hardest thing she'd ever done. She hoped it didn't come to that.

"You know where I'll be," she said, and left.

Rick watched her go, because he couldn't seem to move his feet. He heard the sound of her car engine starting. Then she drove away.

He wasn't sure how long he stood in the foyer of

his house, listening to the silence. He wasn't sure of anything.

Now what? The question echoed in his head. He told himself he would get on with his life. That things would be as they were before. This…interlude with Mandy had been interesting, but nothing more. They could never have made it. As for her loving him, she had demonstrated her feelings by walking away as soon as she declared them. Nothing had changed— certainly not her.

But he didn't believe those words. Not completely. He remembered her statement that this time she wasn't running from something but to something. To Eva.

Then he closed his eyes and imagined a blond little girl laughing as she played, and her redheaded mother watching over her. He thought of how right they looked together. How full their lives would be. How much they would love each other. And he ached.

"Why are you crying?" Eva asked from her place under the umbrella.

Mandy quickly wiped her face and smiled. "I'm not. Well, not very much."

"Are you sad?"

"No. I'll be fine." She smiled at Eva, then adjusted the girl's sun hat.

They sat on the sand in front of the beach house. Cassie was finally due to arrive in the next day or so. Mandy had officially become Eva's foster parent and she'd nearly finished filling out the reams of adoption paperwork the caseworker had given her. Everything was going really, really well. Everything except for the fact that it had been four days and she hadn't heard a word from Rick.

Just thinking about him made her eyes tear, so she forced herself to think about something else. About the bedroom furniture she was going to get for Eva, and how her father had called from France and been delighted at the thought of having a granddaughter to spoil. She'd had to make him promise there would be no surprise ponies showing up at her front door.

So she would be fine. Even if Rick didn't come to his senses. If he didn't know what he had in her, then he was an idiot and she was better off without him.

She knew she was right, but all the logic in her heart didn't heal the ache inside.

"Mandy, look!" Eva called, sitting up and pointing.

Mandy turned and saw a man with a puppy. The sun was in her eyes, so she couldn't see more than his silhouette. She wanted to believe there was something familiar about him, but she'd already tricked herself about a hundred times. She was getting tired of the disappointment.

Then Eva squealed and jumped to her feet.

"Rick, Rick," she called as she ran. "Have you got a puppy?"

Rick?

Mandy stood slowly, unable to believe, not sure what it meant. The man walked close enough for her to see his face. Her heart stood still for a second before thundering into double-time. Eva raced closer and he caught her up in his arms. They spoke for a few seconds, then she crowed with delight. He put her down and she and the puppy tumbled together.

Rick crossed the sand to stand in front of her. He

reached up and pulled off his sunglasses, bent low and kissed her mouth.

"I'm sorry," he said when he straightened. "About a lot of things."

She couldn't speak; she could barely breathe. Instead she stared at him and waited for him to go on.

"I've been thinking about what you said. I've finally figured it all out." He touched her face. "You were right about a lot of it. You were wrong some, too."

Despite the fear, and the hope, she couldn't help smiling. "That's so like you."

"Isn't it?" He touched her cheek. "The thing is, I love you. I'm beginning to think I never stopped loving you. I couldn't seem to fall for anyone else, and I never knew why. It wasn't about needing closure. The problem was I'd given my heart away and had yet to get it back. Now I don't want it back. I want you to keep it."

She felt more tears in her eyes, but these were tears of happiness.

"I know there's no sure thing," he continued. "I've needed it in the past, but now I'm okay with letting that go. What I want now is you and me together. I want us to adopt Eva and have some kids of our own. I want our lives to intertwine until we can't figure out where one ends and the other begins. The sure thing I want is knowing you'll always be there for me, and that you expect the same from me. Sometimes it will be easy and sometimes it will be hard. I want us to accept that, because we only make sense when we're together."

She threw herself into his arms. "Oh, Rick. I love you so much."

"I'm glad." He cupped her face. "Marry me, Mandy. Marry me again. This time, I swear I'll get it right."

"Me, too." She wiped away her tears and smiled at him. "I'll never run away again. I've finally figured out my place is with you."

They embraced, then he kissed her. Eva and her new puppy ran over and bumped into them. Rick bent down and gathered the little girl in his arms. Nothing had ever felt as right as this moment. They were all where they belonged.

COURTING CASSANDRA

Teresa Southwick

Dear Reader,

I grew up in California. My parents had a condo a block from the beach in Carpinteria, a charming resort town just south of Santa Barbara. During the summer, I spent a lot of time there. Many of my favorite memories include reading on the beach.

California is also where I met Susan Mallery. We took a class together on writing romance. She sat in the front row; I was in the back. Always prolific, she was writing more than her critique group could handle. She started another group and asked me to join and an enduring friendship was born. Eventually Susan sold a book to Silhouette Special Edition. And another. And another. I think she'd have to do the math to calculate the total. And I sold to the Romance line at Silhouette. I'm enormously pleased and proud to be a part of it.

But with stories to tell that demand a longer length, I was finally able to break into Special Edition. When Susan and I were brainstorming this book, I casually mentioned that I'd always wanted to set a book in Carpinteria. With that we were off and running. I know it's December. But what better time to let your imagination sweep you away to sand, sea and—most important—sun.

I want to thank our editor, Karen Taylor Richman, for giving us the opportunity to do a book together and for always pushing us to dig deeper into the characters for maximum emotional impact. My gratitude to Susan Mallery, for teaming with me on this project and most especially, for always being there. And to all the Special Edition authors, my appreciation for the stories that still give me many happy hours of reading on the beach. Keep it up! I'm delighted to join your ranks.

And last but by no means least, I'm indebted to the readers. I hope you enjoy Cassie and Kyle's story and look for my debut Special Edition title—*Midnight, Moonlight & Miracles*, available next month.

All the best,

Teresa Southwick

Chapter One

"No good deed goes unpunished," Cassandra Brightwell muttered.

With the outside hose, she rinsed the paintbrush she'd just used, then swiped her fingers down her cheek. When she saw the paint on her hand, she knew it was smeared across her face. Then her idly spoken words sank in and she cringed. Not because she'd been talking to herself, although it was reason enough. But because if the statement was true, a happening of monumental badness was in her immediate future.

Again assuming the statement to be true, what in heaven's name had possessed her to do *two* good deeds? Deed number one: graciously letting her best friend Mandy Carter off the hook. They'd planned to spend a couple of weeks together at the beach house that summer. But Mandy had patched up her relationship with Rick Benson, the love of her life, and would rather be with him than hang with Cassie. Go figure.

Deed number two: abandoned by said best friend, Cassie had decided to paint the Brightwell half of the duplex and complete the makeover her mother had started with the order of new furniture.

Cassie shook her head. "Two good deeds. Not particularly bright for a Brightwell."

Then a red convertible BMW slowly passed her and pulled into the driveway that mirrored her own. She instantly recognized the driver and cringed again.

Kyle Stratton. When she saw the beautiful brunette in the passenger seat, she prayed for her own personal tsunami to sweep her out to sea. The Stratton family owned the other half of the duplex and had spent summers there along with the Brightwells. Kyle was still her brother Dan's best friend.

The two of them, along with Cassie and Megan Brightwell and Kyle's sister, Amy, had hung out together. She still considered him a good friend, even after their one and only date had cranked up her unrequited crush, then let her down with a resounding thud.

Until recently, Cassie had lived in Phoenix, so she only saw him when she visited for holidays or summer vacation—her semiannual exposure to and reinfection of what she called the Kyle crush.

CRUSH—all capitals. What an appropriate word. Her tender feelings for him had certainly been crushed into many small pieces. Afterward, she'd carefully put them away—like dried basil in a plastic seasonings container relegated to the darkest, almost forgotten recesses of the pantry. It was best not to harbor false hope, to keep their relationship strictly as friends. He already treated her like a kid sister. No point in giving him a good laugh at her expense.

Her experience with Kyle, or nonexperience depending on one's interpretation, should have made her cautious about taking another chance on romance. But not Cassie Brightwell. *Good* deeds weren't the only things she did in twos.

But that was all history. She was over her crush on Kyle.

As usual, Kyle looked like one of the top ten on the list of the fifty most beautiful people as he got out of the car and stretched. Before she could stop it, her heart skipped at the sight of him. He was tall—six feet if she remembered correctly. Who was she kidding? She could never quite forget anything about Kyle. Including his profession.

In his long-sleeved white dress shirt, dark-brown slacks and loosened striped tie in shades of gold and chocolate, he looked every inch the wildly successful, hotshot divorce attorney he was. His hair, dark brown and cut stylishly short, was dashingly windblown. Cassie couldn't see his eyes behind his trendy sunglasses, but she knew they were brown—puppy-dog eyes.

He walked to the passenger side of the car then opened the door for the woman with him. Was it too late to head for the hills? Maybe he hadn't seen her. No such luck. As Cassie considered slipping inside the duplex, his gaze met hers. He stared hard at her for a moment, then smiled, waved and moved toward her.

She'd been made. The irony didn't escape her. All those times she'd prayed he would notice her in a different way. How bad was her luck that he would start noticing her now when she was covered in paint? It was that second good deed. She jotted down a mental note to cease and desist all good deeds immediately.

Accompanied by his female passenger, he stopped on the sidewalk in front of her. "Cassie Brightwell."

"Kyle Stratton, as I live and breathe."

Although that last part was questionable. The exchange of oxygen and carbon dioxide wasn't happening very efficiently with her lungs suddenly unable to take in air. Standing this close to him was dangerous to her health.

"How long has it been?" he asked.

"Probably Christmas holidays when I was in from Phoenix. Who's your friend?" She tried to make her tone as charming and Scarlett O'Hara-like as her "live and breathe" remark.

"Oh. Sorry." He glanced at the woman beside him. "Beth Deveraux, this is Cassie Brightwell."

"Dan's little sister?" the woman asked. "He didn't tell me you looked like Gwyneth Paltrow."

"If only. Besides, my brother's not exactly a font of information. Then there's the whole forgotten-middle-child thing." When the woman stared at her with a blank expression, Cassie added, "Older brother, Dan, younger sister, Megan. I'm the one in the middle everybody forgets."

"Ah," Beth said simply.

"By the way, how do you know my brother?"

"They met once or twice at my office," Kyle explained. "Beth is a client of mine."

So *that's* what he was calling it these days. "Kyle is your attorney?"

Beth nodded, tucking a wind blown shoulder-length strand of reddish brown hair behind her ear. "The best. My ex-husband found that out the hard way."

"So are you two here for the weekend?" Cassie asked, praying he would say no.

This was supposed to be *her* vacation. She'd planned down time, a chance to relax before starting the demanding new job that had brought her back to California. At least she told herself it was the job and not the shock of her fiancé's betrayal that had brought her back. Once the decision had been made, she'd decided it was an opportunity for a do-over. She was determined to live life to the fullest and without regrets.

Now that she was here, the last thing she'd expected was Kyle and his latest arm candy, bimbo queen of the valley, cuddling and snuggling and doing other stuff she didn't want to know about on the other side of the shared wall between the duplexes.

He rested his hands on his lean hips. "Beth hitched a ride with me. Her boyfriend lives in Santa Barbara. He should be here any minute to pick her up."

And what a lovely woman she was, Cassie thought.

No sooner had Kyle explained the boyfriend, than a sporty two-seater Mercedes pulled up to the curb.

"I told you he was good." Beth leaned over and kissed his cheek—without standing on tiptoe. "Thanks for everything, Kyle. Nice to meet you, Cassie. Bye."

She wiggled her fingers, then turned away, hips doing a sexy sway, heels clicking on the sidewalk as she went to meet the man waiting for her. Cassie watched the car make a U-turn and drive back up palm-tree-lined Linden Avenue.

Kyle looked down at her. "So, how are things in Phoenix? Are you here on vacation?"

"Dan didn't tell you I was moving back to California?"

He shook his head. "Don't recall him mentioning it. Did you finally get tired of living on the face of the sun?"

It had been hot—and she wasn't just talking about the weather. But her make-Kyle-think-twice-about-ignoring-her fantasy had never included sharing details of her recent romantic ruin. She had two major regrets, double motivation for her decision to live life to the fullest. Number one regret—agreeing to share her Phoenix apartment with Lynnda Bradley-Simmons, the she-devil of the planet. Regret number two—introducing Steve Turner, her fiancé, and a man who didn't know the meaning of the word *loyalty*, to her roommate.

She smiled up at Kyle. "I was offered a great job at Valley General Hospital. Too good to turn down."

"Congratulations. I was beginning to think maybe you'd abandoned nursing and taken up a new profession," he said, reaching out to brush the smudge of paint from her nose.

Damn. She hated the tingles dancing over her skin on account of his touch. She told herself it was only the sea breeze, but stepped back anyway.

"Nursing pays better than volunteer painting. Mandy Carter and I had planned to spend a month here, to catch up on old times. But I got hung up in Phoenix. My two weeks' notice turned into a four-week mercy mission to train my replacement. When I finally got here, Mandy had to leave. I decided to keep busy and give the duplex a coat of paint. What are you doing here?'' she asked.

One second a shadow flashed across his face, the next it was gone. It happened so quickly she wondered if she'd imagined the response.

He crossed his arms over his chest. ''I'm taking some time off.''

''And you're taking it here in Carpinteria?''

''Yeah. Why?''

She shrugged. ''I just thought you'd vacation at the current trendy spot.''

''It's not a vacation.''

''It should be,'' she said. ''You look terrible.''

''Thank you very much.''

''Sorry. I could have been a shade more diplomatic.''

He shook his head. ''Honesty is a rare quality these days. Rare and brutal,'' he said, one corner of his wonderful mouth turning up.

The attempt at a smile didn't fool her. She studied him, really looked beyond what she remembered and took in what was there now. A muscle in his lean cheek moved tensely. Deep grooves bracketed his nose and mouth. He looked tired.

She squeezed more water from her paintbrush. ''I was planning to take a walk on the beach. Would you care to join me?''

''Yeah.''

''Okay. Give me a few minutes to clean up and make myself presentable. I wouldn't want you to have to walk ten paces behind because you're embarrassed to be seen with me.''

''With those short legs, you couldn't stay that far ahead of me,'' he said, laughing.

"The short jokes were annoying when we were kids. They're going to crash and burn now that we're adults."

"Okay. Your protest is noted and filed."

"Good. See you in a few."

"As soon as I slip into something more comfortable."

The words—cliché for let's do the horizontal hopscotch—were innocent and had nothing to do with her, but Cassie didn't know how to get that message to her wildly skipping pulse. She would have a better chance of flapping her arms and flying to the moon than getting Kyle Stratton to say something like that to her. And she didn't want him to. Not really. She just wanted to dazzle him with all her clothes on and make him wish he'd paid more attention to her when he'd had the chance.

With Cassie beside him, Kyle stepped off the sidewalk and into the sand. "Which way do you want to go?"

She glanced left, then right and shielded her eyes from the sun with her hand. "Left."

He nodded and they trudged through the hot, loose sand to the darker hard-packed stuff by the ocean. As the waves broke on shore and rolled onto the beach, they dodged the water when it rushed up faster than expected. Cassie had changed into a T-shirt and sweatpants. A matching fleece top was tied around her neck. She'd pulled her just-below-shoulder-length blond hair to the top of her head. With her face free of makeup, she looked around twelve. But all the curves between her slender neck and shapely ankles told him it was a lie.

Kyle had shed his own work clothes and put on shorts and a T-shirt. If only he could shed other concerns as easily. But there was something about coming back to the beach house. He didn't have many good childhood memories, but most, if not all of the good ones, were tied up in this place. And the Brightwells.

"So what made you decide to come here for your time off?" Cassie asked, breaking their companionable silence.

Always, his first instinct was to gloss over everything. For some reason he didn't choose to now.

"I wanted to think about things."

"Care to be more specific?"

"Evaluate my life."

"Care to be more specific?" she asked again, tilting her head to look up at him.

"To quote my mother, I've been crabby, cranky and a couple other things she's too much of a lady to say. She suggested I come up here, get in touch with my roots and figure out why I've been so ornery."

"Have you come up with anything yet?"

"I got here forty minutes ago," he answered wryly.

"Oh. Yeah. But you always were a gifted overachiever."

"Not this time. I'm evaluating the offer of a partnership in the firm."

"Kyle, that's great. Congratulations."

"Thanks."

"What took you so long?" Although she shielded her eyes from the sun, mischief lurked in their depths.

"It took me a while to figure out where I wanted to specialize. Considering that, it actually happened quickly."

"So they've obviously recognized your genius. I'm not exactly sure what you've got to evaluate. But maybe I could help—be your sounding board."

He glanced at her and could have sworn the vibrancy emanating from her actually touched him. She was a small woman and a sensation of protectiveness for her swept over him. Along with something else that sent blood racing through his veins, pooling south of his belt line when a sweet smile made the corners of her wide mouth curve upward. The warmth spread to her big, bright blue eyes. He'd known her since they were kids and he had to admit she'd filled out nicely in all the right places. He was no carpenter and didn't work with wood, but he couldn't imagine anyone who looked less like a board.

"Sounding board? As in be my shrink?" he asked.

"As in being your friend. Look, if it would make you feel better, we'll set a time limit." She stared down the beach and pointed. "See that big rock formation? You only have to talk about yourself until we get there. Deal?"

"It's not far. Okay," he agreed. "That was pretty fair negotiating. You should have been a lawyer."

"Not on your life. Lawyers are life's bottom-feeders and divorce—"

"Attorneys are the bottomest of the bottom?" He watched her tug on the corner of her lip with her teeth. "Don't stop now. You're on a roll."

"I seem to have inadvertently hit a hot button."

"The general public sees my profession as a downer, the butt of jokes. I'll admit that I see the worst part of a relationship—the bitter end."

"Your profession isn't a downer."

"Nice of you to say that. But it's my job to make

sure the other guy gives up as much as possible. Sometimes it goes easy, sometimes not and I get a lottery of billable hours. In a divorce situation, I'm the only winner.''

''If you really believe that, why did you go into divorce law?''

''My dad once told me there are three things you can count on in life. Death, taxes and relationship meltdown.''

''So you specialized in divorces for the money?'' she asked.

He shook his head. ''I wanted to prevent people like my dad being taken to the cleaners. Mom got the house, the duplex here at the beach and pretty much all of the terms she wanted as part of her divorce settlement. Since then, I've lost track of how many times Mom and Dad have remarried and divorced. He made the remark recently that he would never have anything as long as he was with a woman.''

''Did you tell him he should pick someone his own age with similar interests who can tolerate his penchant for self-absorption?'' she asked sweetly.

''It never occurred to me.'' Although it was damn good advice. Obviously she knew a thing or two about his father.

''First, it doesn't take a mental giant to see why you picked the law specialty you did. You're trying to save your family over and over again—with every client you represent.''

He laughed. ''Oh, please.''

''Think about it,'' she said. ''Every man or woman who hires you becomes your mother or father and you're trying to protect them.''

''Way too noble, not to mention just plain weird.

And for God's sake, don't make me out to be more than I am."

"I'm not going to argue with you. It's irrelevant to my point, and I do have one. I sense that you're no longer getting satisfaction from your profession."

"I take satisfaction from the fact that I'm good at what I do. I know the law. What's that saying? You have to know the rules before you can break them."

"You break the law?" she asked.

"Of course not. I manipulate it. I'm committed to doing the best I can for my client. I like the challenge, the give-and-take battle. It's like a chess game—move and countermove. When I win, it's exhilarating."

"I'm guessing you win often or they wouldn't be offering you a partnership." She stopped walking suddenly and turned to him. "You're not thinking of turning it down, are you?"

"I'm not stupid," he said wryly. He stuck his hands in his pockets and they started walking again. "The offer felt like a turning point for me and seemed to stimulate some personal reflection. I just thought there would be more."

"Are we talking professionally or personally?"

"Take your pick."

Looking straight ahead, she said, "I can't comment on your personal life, but in case you're having a crisis of conscience about what you do for a living, rest assured it's very necessary. You're the rose between two thorns."

"I'm not especially comfortable being compared to a rose, but thanks. I guess."

"Think about it. Two people on opposite sides, warring. Prickly. The thorns. At such a volatile time, a couple needs someone objective, someone with a clear head. The rose," she said. "Divorce is an unfortunate and ugly fact of life. Your skill is essential, especially when there are children involved."

"I'm a well-paid referee."

"No. Expert representation. You said yourself that you know the law. I wouldn't call it manipulation that you're aware of every protection it provides."

He glanced at her until she met his gaze. "What happened to the whole 'lawyers as bottom feeders' thing?"

"I was kidding."

"Okay. I guess I didn't recognize it, because who knew Florence Nightingale had such a sarcastic sense of humor."

"Oh puhleeze. I'm no Florence N."

"But you are a nurse. I admire what you do. Working to make sick people better. I bet you're very good at it."

"Easy for you to say. You already know I was offered a job that's a big step up."

"Yeah, but knowing you, I feel they've chosen wisely."

"Since when are you a shameless flatterer?"

"The truth is never shameless nor is it flattery."

"We're supposed to be talking about you," she said. "So how's your love life?"

"That was blunt."

"No, merely curious. You're here to evaluate your life, and there's more to it than work. Since we already talked about the work portion, there's still the other part."

"Time flies when you're having fun." He pointed to the rock formation they'd seen from far away that now seemed to appear out of nowhere to signal he was off the hook. "How fortuitous I don't have to talk about myself anymore. But speaking of love life…I seem to remember Dan telling me you're engaged."

All too well Kyle recalled his reaction to the news. He'd felt as if his best friend had sucker punched him. Stupid really, because he and Cassie would never be a twosome. Her brother had made that clear a long time ago. If Kyle asked Cassie out, his friendship with Dan was over.

At the time, the choice had been a no-brainer. Dan was the best friend he'd ever had, the one who was always there for him, the one he could count on above everyone else—including his own parents. Kyle couldn't chance having no one. After that, whenever he saw Cassie, he ignored her. Over the years, it had become harder to do that. She'd changed from a plain, skinny girl into a beautiful woman—inside and out.

"When's the wedding?" he prompted.

"When hell freezes over."

"Don't sugarcoat it, Cass. Tell me how you really feel."

"We broke up."

"What happened?"

"I don't want to talk about it."

"Interesting how the rules change when you're on the psychiatrist's couch," he commented.

"I'm not the one who's here to evaluate my life. I'm the one who's here to spend time with her best friend who found something better to do and stood her up."

"So you're between significant others?"

"I'll tell you about mine if you tell me about yours," she offered.

"I don't have one."

"Me, either."

Kyle didn't realize he was holding his breath until he was forced to suck air into his lungs. And the strange feeling that boulders the size of Texas were lifted from his shoulders—was that relief?

"You expect me to believe you're not involved with someone?" she asked.

"I don't expect anything. It's the truth."

"You always have a Barbie, Bambi or Brandi with an *i* in your life. Come to think of it, I thought Dan said *you* were engaged."

"I was. I came to my senses and broke it off."

"Cold feet?"

"Yeah." He glanced at her. "You look surprised. Is it that I had cold feet or because I was engaged?"

She shook her head. "I'm shocked you *admitted* to cold feet. Although, I don't know why I should be. It's not a stretch. Everyone knows you're commitment phobic."

"Is that so?"

"I've heard through the grapevine—aka Dan Brightwell—that you've told more than one aspiring Mrs. Kyle Stratton not to expect more than a physical relationship. And I never saw you bring the same woman around twice."

"Twice implies a pledge to the future."

"I rest my case. You don't want to get married."

Odd, he didn't mind talking to her about all this. Maybe because she knew his history. She'd been there through the ups and downs. Or maybe it was because she was *safe*.

"It's not marriage I object to. It's the divorce when it doesn't work out. I don't want to end up broke like my old man, or going through the relationship revolving door like Mom.''

"What about kids?''

"What about them?''

"Don't you like children?'' she asked.

"I like them very much.''

"Me, too. I can't imagine my life without children.''

"In spite of being the forgotten middle child? Even after what your sister Megan went through with Bayleigh?''

"The problem with Bayleigh's eyes isn't genetic. And, by the way she's doing fine since her transplant. But that isn't the point. Megan loved her daughter's father and the guy walked out on her because of Bayleigh's health problems. But she wouldn't change anything if it meant not having her child. I want to be a mom more than anything.''

And she would make a wonderful mother, he thought. All she had to do was pick the right man. He recalled offering to bring Bayleigh's father back and make him pay support. Dan had suggested a well-placed fist, but Megan had nixed all the ideas. She'd said the jerk was being punished enough. He was missing out on a relationship with his daughter and the privilege of watching her grow up.

Kyle looked at Cassie. "Would you still want to be a mom if you had to raise the child alone like Megan's doing?''

"It's not my first choice. What about you? How would you feel about raising a child alone?''

"What you really want to know is if I want to have any kids—period. And the answer is no.''

Cassie couldn't have looked more shocked if he'd

dropped his shorts and hollered, "Nude beach."
"Don't you feel the need to have a child to carry on
the Stratton name?"

"No."

"Why not?"

He stopped walking and picked up a smooth stone,
then tossed it sidearm into the ocean. "It should be
obvious to someone who's known me as long as you
have."

"I'm slow. Spell it out for me," she said, hands
on hips.

"Okay. You always complained about being the
forgotten middle child—not the oldest or the youn-
gest. The one in the middle who wasn't special in any
way."

"Yeah. So?"

"I was just forgotten. My parents were too busy
separating, dating, marrying, divorcing and separating—not necessarily in that order—to give a damn
about me. Don't you remember that Christmas Dan
brought me home from school with him because they
each thought I was with the other one and they were
both out of the country?"

"I remember him bringing you home. I don't know
if I knew why." She met his gaze. "You need to take
a page from Megan's book. It was your parents'
loss."

Debatable, he thought. "After that, I spent most
holidays with your family." He studied her, the
clouds in her eyes blocking out the earlier brightness.

"Is there a point to this trip down memory lane?
Other than whining? In case you didn't recognize it
just now, that was tough love."

"Is that how you help your patients?"

"If that's what they need," she answered.

"That wasn't whining, merely an explanation for why I wouldn't be a good parent. I pity any kid who got me for a father. He'd best be prepared to raise himself."

"That's ridiculous. I've seen you with Bayleigh. You're wonderful with her."

"It's easy to look good on a short-term basis. But twenty-four seven?" He shook his head. "It doesn't take a Ph.D. in child rearing to know the seeds of parenting are sown in childhood. Based on that, I have no training. My folks were never around."

"Then it's a good thing you spent a lot of time at my house, hanging out with Dan," she added.

"He's my best friend. I'd do anything for Dan."

"Including being a mercy escort for his little sister so the two of you could double-date?"

He knew right away what she was referring to. About ten years ago, Kyle and Dan had been home from college. Their alma mater was in the football playoffs. Dan had a date for the game and wanted Kyle to ask someone. He'd come up empty on such short notice and the two of them had talked Cassie into going along. It had been one of the best nights he could remember.

"It wasn't a mercy date," he said.

"Then why didn't you call me again?"

Chapter Two

Under normal circumstances, Cassie would have wanted to disappear after saying something so bold. But this was the new-and-improved Cassie, the one determined to not have any regrets. She wasn't exactly sure how his aversion to having children had segued into her question, but she refused to regret it.

In her head, she understood his reasons were firmly rooted in his unstable childhood environment. In her heart, the idea of Kyle all alone made her inexplicably sad. If she couldn't have kids, she knew there would be a hole the size of the Grand Canyon in her life.

She'd always thought the instinct to procreate irrepressible. Of course with Kyle it was all about sex. She'd heard her brother say more than once Kyle was a playboy. When he got what he wanted from a woman, he walked away. That's what had prompted her question. He hadn't gotten anything from her and maybe it was time to find out why.

Why didn't you call me again?

Or maybe it was time to head into the sun. She did an abrupt about-face. "I have to go back now. Feel free to keep going in the other direction," she called over her shoulder. "Smooth, Brightwell," she muttered to herself.

"A gentleman always escorts a lady home." Kyle fell into step beside her.

"Really? And where did the man raised by wolves learn that?" She hoped that would distract him from her last question.

He squinted into the sun as he thought. "From my father actually."

"So he was around at least once."

"Apparently." He took her arm to steady her as she stumbled over a rock half-submerged in the sand. "Are you sure I never called you?"

"Positive. And I distinctly remember you promised to."

She'd stayed home waiting for his call, certain it would happen the next day. It didn't. After that, she'd slept with the phone, eaten with it as her companion, studied with it staring at her. She even took it with her when she showered. Her mother joked about having it surgically removed from her hand and the behavior had continued for a month or more. Until Dan had let it slip that Kyle was dating yet another girl he'd met in college. A regular Casanova. And the news had broken Cassie's eighteen-year-old heart. Oh, yeah, she was sure he'd never called.

He looked down at her and reached over to remove a strand of hair from her eyes and tuck it behind her ear. "It was important to keep my grades up to get in to law school. I must have been busy studying."

"I bet you were. Female anatomy."

Frowning, Kyle stuck his hands in his pockets. "It was for the best, Cass."

He didn't even bother to deny it one more time. She should have let it drop. There wasn't a decent reason to put herself through this. Then she realized that was wrong. She had a very good reason. The question hadn't come out of nowhere. She'd always wondered. One of her most profound regrets was that she'd never confronted him about it. After her disastrous romance in Phoenix, she'd promised herself a new start in California. That included no more regrets.

"Whose best was it for?" Certainly not hers. She would always wonder what might have been. "I asked Dan about it and he wouldn't say anything."

"I'm not the kind of guy your bro— Your family wouldn't want you to get mixed up with someone like me."

Pressure started in her chest and grew to an ache deep inside her. He'd all but admitted he'd ignored her on purpose, which put her smack dab in the emotional abyss she'd experienced ten years ago.

And who was he to decide what her family wanted? Her mother and father thought he walked on water. Megan was half in love with him and Dan was his best friend. Which Brightwell didn't want her involved with him?

"Oh, really. You make a decent living, you're not bad looking, and you have an above-average trendy car. What's not to like?"

"You deserve someone better, Cass."

"Isn't that for me to decide?" Although her last choice hadn't been especially smart.

"We don't always know what's best for us."

Then a worse thought occurred to her. She'd always felt she and Kyle had connected on that date all those years ago. Instinct had told her they'd gone a step above friendship before he'd pulled back. But maybe he was a good actor. Maybe the whole evening had been tedious and he was embarrassed to be seen in public with her. Maybe he didn't want to come right out and say he couldn't care about her if she was the last woman on earth. Maybe he was trying not to hurt her feelings. If so, she needed to know. She'd already wasted enough of her life mooning over Kyle. It was past time for a booster shot.

"Did you want to call me or not?" she asked.

He glanced down at her, then to his left, and pointed to the large rock formation they passed for the second time. "As per our previous verbal contract, I am no longer obligated to talk about me."

It wasn't just about him. And now that she'd raised the question, she felt as if she couldn't drop it. She also sensed she wasn't going to get an answer. At least not now.

"Very slick, Counselor. Have it your way. In fact I don't want to talk about you anymore. You're pretty boring."

"No kidding." He laughed.

"I wasn't joking."

An uneasy silence slipped over them as they walked along the shore. They were almost back to their starting place when a particularly large wave broke and rushed up, catching Cassie off guard. It washed over her feet and wet her sweatpants to the knee.

"Mercy, that's cold," she shrieked, pulling the elastic hem up. "My ankles hurt."

"Wimp."

"Them's fightin' words." She was still miffed about the way he'd shut down and refused to talk. Raising her hands, she curled her fingers into fists, then bobbed and weaved in front of him.

Without warning, Kyle scooped her up in his arms. "I don't have to fight. All I have to do is throw you in the ocean. And I can because I'm bigger."

"You wouldn't." All the same, she wrapped her arms around his neck and held on, meeting his amused gaze. "If I go in, so do you."

"Is that a dare?"

"What if it is?"

"I never could resist a dare."

She leaned to the side, looked at the water and back up at him. "Then, of course it isn't a dare. Now put me down, please."

"As the lady wishes." He made a sudden move as if he was going to drop her.

She squealed and gripped him tighter. "You are going to hell, Kyle Stratton. Now put me down."

She'd never meant anything less. If she'd known it felt so good to be in his arms, she'd have let him throw her in the ocean a long time ago. Over and over. Just for the brief pleasure of having him hold her. She was so pathetic.

"I suppose down means dry land?" he asked.

"Please," she managed to say.

"Spoilsport," he mumbled as he set her on her feet and held on to her arm until she was steady.

The touch of his fingers on her bare skin scorched her clear down to her soul. If she ever saw his mother, she would be sure *not* to thank her for sending him here. Her intention to spend time at the summer house hadn't included a painful trip down memory lane. She was angry with him, but more annoyed with herself for bringing it up in the first place.

"It's time I was getting back," she said.

"Got a hot date?"

She laughed. "I just moved back. I don't work as fast as the legendary Kyle Stratton."

"I'm not fast."

"That's not what I heard," she scoffed. "For you and my brother the duplex is like seduction central."

They trudged back through the sand to the sidewalk and headed up Linden Avenue.

"What have you heard?"

"Rumor has it that within minutes of meeting a woman, you can charm a phone number and a date, usually at your place, where seduction and dinner, not necessarily in that order, soon follow."

"Dan's lying."

"About him or you? I'm curious about the step-by-step process you guys use to get from point A to point B with a woman."

He slid her a wry look. "I'm not going to dignify that statement with a response. Suffice it to say tales of my—our—exploits are grossly exaggerated."

"And I'm not going to dignify that with a retort."

Thank goodness, they were finally back. At the bottom of the duplex stairs, Cassie tried to stomp the sand from her feet, but it was wet and sticky. Not wanting to track it inside, she grabbed the hose and turned on the water to rinse her feet.

"Hey, I need some of that, too," Kyle said, glancing down.

Cassie looked at the hose, then at him, and couldn't resist. She turned up the water, then aimed the nozzle in his direction, soaking him.

"Hey!" he cried, holding up his hands. "That's cold!"

"You said you needed some cold water."

Not that a cooling off from time spent with her was necessary. Apparently she was eminently resistible and the only one whose body temperature urgently needed lowering. She leveled the stream of water at his face.

He put his hands up. "I'm warning you, Cass—"

"Devil made me do it," she said, backing away as he took a step toward her.

He lunged forward. Battling past the spray, he easily wrestled the hose away from her, dousing her from head to toe in retaliation.

"Uncle," she cried, turning her back. "I give up."

"Loser has to fix dinner."

She glanced over her shoulder. He was shutting off the water, so she pivoted toward him. "Are you implying there was some sort of contest to which I admitted defeat and now I have to pay up?"

"Yeah."

He straightened and she stood in front of him, squeezing the excess water out of her sopping ponytail. "First of all, I'm not a loser. I simply decided to stop fighting. Second, when there's a wager, it has to be verbalized ahead of time. I didn't invite you to dinner."

"Then let me invite myself."

"Okay." She was so pathetically easy. But this was also an opportunity. "But there are conditions."

"Name them."

"Only two. The first, we keep it simple. Barbecue steaks and throw together a salad?"

"Done."

"Second, you provide a simple demonstration of the Stratton seduction style—how you get from point A to point B with a woman."

He shook his head and droplets of water sparkled like diamonds in his dark hair then fell on his already soaked shirt. If there was a male wet-T-shirt contest, he would win hands down. The impressive muscles of his chest and harnessed strength in his upper arms were clearly outlined.

"Uh-uh. No way."

Cassie's cheeks burned. Humiliation wasn't any easier now than it had been all those years ago. But this time she had maturity on her side and wasn't willing to roll over and forget it. This was the new Cassie who didn't want to wake up tomorrow and be sorry she hadn't pushed the advantage when she'd had it. She'd opened a can of worms with her question. Maybe because it was time to settle the past before she could embrace her future. Bottom line— she wanted to know what she'd missed out on.

"I'm not saying go all the way," she explained, squeezing the water out of her sweatshirt to hide the fact that in spite of her resolve, her hands were shaking nervously. "Just set the mood and tell me what you would do."

"Why?"

She shrugged. "Curiosity. I'd like to know what

you would do—*if* you were attempting to seduce me.''

''If I refuse, does that mean you won't feed me?''
he asked, raising one dark eyebrow.

''Yes.'' She wrung out the hem of her T-shirt, to
minimize her dripping. Then she walked up the stairs
and wiped her bare feet on the welcome mat.

The duplex had a single outside door that opened
into a shared foyer. The Brightwell unit was to the
right and Kyle's to the left. Cassie let herself in and
Kyle followed. She unlocked her unit and opened the
door. Instantly the overpowering smell of paint hit her
and she coughed then waved her hand in front of her
face.

''You need to open the windows and air out the
place,'' Kyle told her.

''You think? Thanks for the tip. That would never
have occurred to me,'' she said.

''Looks like you're going to have to pay that bet
off at my place,'' he said.

''It wasn't a bet. And I'd be happy to have dinner
at your place.'' She smiled up at him. ''And may I
say, nice move. It's just like Dan said. Within
minutes, phone number and dinner at your place. So
begins Seduction 101.''

''Only dinner. A man has to eat. No seduction.''

Cassie chose to ignore him. ''I'll clean up, air out
my place, and be back with the stuff for dinner.''

Anticipation coursing through her, she turned away
from him. Where were the stiletto heels and little
black dress when you really needed them?

''This is a fine mess,'' Kyle muttered to himself.
Cassie would be there any minute and he hoped

her request for a play-by-play on seduction had been forgotten or was nothing more than a joke, because he had a big problem.

From the moment he'd seen her again, in cutoffs, tank top and paint, he'd wanted her in his bed. Walking along the beach with her had been like a stroll down memory lane with his security blanket. It should have put her firmly back in honorary little sister status, but instead had only cranked up his need. Why *hadn't* he called her again?

He'd fought the urge for weeks after taking her to that football game. She'd been fun and funny. For the first time he'd seen her as more than Dan's little sister and he'd felt it could be the start of something big. Until Dan's ultimatum. Losing the friendship wasn't an option—not then, not now.

But seeing Cassie again and hearing her question had stirred up memories, had increased his simmering dissatisfaction. She'd said it herself—he wasn't bad-looking, had a good job, a car, and there was no shortage of women. So why did he feel as if his life was empty, that there should be so much more? The look on her face—in her eyes—when she'd asked why he'd never called her again had made him want to fold her in his arms. The expression was familiar. In the divorce wars one person was nearly always hurt because they loved more. Cassie had the look, a loss of innocence in her eyes, a bruised air as if someone had beaten down her soul. No question about it. Someone had damaged her. The idea of anyone hurting her made him furious. And she'd refused to tell him about her broken engagement, so he had a pretty good idea who. If he ever got his hands on the guy…

But he had a bigger problem at the moment. She'd

requested he tell her about his seduction style. If he started, it wouldn't be just talk. No way was he going there. The only solution was not to play. He should have told her to forget dinner. He could have grabbed a bite alone somewhere or picked up a microwave something. Both ideas were unappealing, but so was the potential for a mess. It wasn't too late to call it off.

There was a soft knock on the door. "Show time," he muttered. "No—not a show. Dinner. Nothing more."

He crossed the tiled floor and opened the door. Cassie stood there, holding a covered bowl with a plate on top that held steaks ready for the grill. "Hi," he said.

"Hi." She walked past him and looked around. "I can't remember the last time I was here. Your mom really fixed up the place. Which is probably where my mom got inspired."

Kyle hadn't noticed. He knew this place was a mirror of the Brightwells, but the decorating was different. There was a stairway just beside the door that led to three bedrooms upstairs. The railing was oak now instead of wrought iron. On the far wall of the living room was a raised-hearth brick fireplace. The chimney went up the outside wall and his mother had added a fireplace in the master bedroom just above. There was a powder room beneath the stairway and the kitchen, separated from the main area by a beige, ceramic-tile-covered bar. Four tall oak swivel stools stood in front of it.

Cassie met his gaze. "My mom said the furniture she ordered is practically indestructible, in a color that will camouflage everything from tar to red punch."

She angled her chin toward the sofa and love seat. "That white furniture is a dead giveaway that this is not a place for kids."

"Welcome to my world," he said. "Let me take that stuff for you."

"Ah, the gentlemanly approach."

"Excuse me?"

"You know. The whole gentleman thing. I'm not sure it works for me. But do you size up a woman then tailor your plan of attack? Sort of a customized, personalized strategy for seduction?"

He groaned inwardly. Apparently it was too much to hope she would have forgotten. "No."

"No, your technique isn't personal?"

"No I'm not going to do this with you."

"Why?"

"You're my best friend's sister. Call it a guy thing. There are lines you don't cross. Besides, you're also my friend."

"So, what does that have to do with anything?"

"It's complicated." He rubbed the back of his neck. "This is just too weird. Can't we talk about sports or the weather?"

"I'm not asking you to compromise your principles. Just tell me what you would do if—"

There was that word again. "If what?"

"If you were with a woman you were attracted to."

If he was attracted? There was a no-brainer. The way she looked tonight, turning back the tide would be easier than keeping his hands off her. Her straight blond hair was loose and tucked behind her ears. He wanted to run his fingers through the strands that looked like silver silk.

She was all in black—jeans and a T-shirt, strappy

sandals revealing red-painted toes. But with her curvy little figure those jeans made his hands ache to get her out of them. And that was no ordinary T-shirt, or should he say half shirt. It was made out of the same soft material, and left one creamy shoulder bare. She wore no jewelry, but it would have paled in comparison to her attributes. No *if* about it. He was damned attracted to her. She had temptation written all over her. Why couldn't she be in a gunnysack with a sign across the front that read No Trespassing?

It was getting hot in here. "Would you like a glass of wine?" he asked, then kicked himself from here to Canada.

"I'd love some." She smiled. "I bet that's step one. Lower your subject's resistance with alcohol."

"They're not subjects. How insensitive do you think I am? Don't answer that."

Debating the wisdom of giving her alcohol, he walked into the kitchen, because he definitely needed some. She followed and set the salad and steak on the counter beside the sink. Kyle riffled through the drawer where his mother kept the foil cutter and cork-screw. After dealing with the bottle he'd brought with him, he pulled a couple glasses from the cupboard and poured the rich red merlot into each.

He handed one to Cassie. "Here. This is just being a good host. Let's deal with dinner. I'll start the fire."

Actually it was already started and burning him to a crisp from inside out. But there was a limit to what he'd tell her.

"I thought I was supposed to cook."

"Don't bite the hand that feeds you."

If he didn't do something to occupy his hands, he would fill them with her. A disaster in the making.

She sipped her wine, then asked, "Do you usually achieve your goal before dinner or after?"

"What?"

Humor danced in her blue eyes and her tempting mouth curved in a mysterious smile. "Statistically, I mean. Rough estimate. Just a ballpark figure."

"What's with you?" He folded his arms over his chest.

She leaned back against the counter, holding her wineglass in both hands. There was about a foot between them. "For a long time I've heard about the romantic exploits of Dan Brightwell. Megan and I had questions, but he would never answer. You and Dan are friends. Do you have the same technique? Compare notes? I'm curious."

"Curiosity killed the cat."

"Maybe. And maybe if Dan had talked to me I'd be content. Or maybe if you'd called me like you said you would…"

She was killing him. He hadn't wanted to be alone tonight, which was why he'd manipulated this dinner. But who knew she would push all his hot buttons? What was going on with her?

No. He didn't want to know the answer. He was afraid if he found out it would cost him more than he could afford to pay.

"This was a bad idea," he said. "If your place isn't aired out enough, you can stay here. I'll find a hotel in Santa Barbara."

"What?" Her playful expression disappeared. "I thought we were friends."

"We are."

"Then why would you leave?"

She had him there. If he ran, she would know the

reason why—he didn't trust himself to be alone with her.

Then he made a calculated error. He looked into her eyes. The bruised expression was back—black and blue. Some other guy had put it there first, but he couldn't pile on. The idea of hurting her was like tossing a defenseless kitten out in the cold. He couldn't bring himself to do it.

Kyle knew he didn't have a lot of choices and figured the best defense was a strong offense. Two could play this game and he was pretty sure he played it better.

"Okay, friend. You win. You've got a front row seat for seduction, Stratton style."

Chapter Three

Friend? Cassie's pulse tap-danced as Kyle moved in front of her. Would someone who was simply a friend notice the heat of his body through the material of his charmingly rumpled cotton shirt and shorts? He'd only moved a foot, yet he'd managed to completely alter her definition of the word *friendship* at the same time he revved up her sense of anticipation. Then he placed his hands on either side of her on the counter, trapping her between his muscular arms. His wrists grazed her arms.

"Well. O-okay," she said. "I'm glad you finally see things my way. Now I've got you right where I want you—"

One corner of his mouth curved upward. "Yes?"

"I guess the question is what am I going to do with you?"

"That's a good question."

"I have a better one."

"Okay."

"What are you going to do with me?" She swallowed. "Let me rephrase. Wh-what's your next move?"

Without actually moving his hand, he managed to caress her forearm with his thumb, sending goose bumps racing over her skin. Her insides turned into a quivering, shivering mess. She held her wineglass between them as if it was a shield.

"This is my next move." Kyle reached up and took her glass, setting it on the counter beside them.

Actually that was the one after his next move, because she was still struggling to maintain her composure from the devastation of his thumb caress. "Why did you take my wine? Doesn't that make your work here easier?"

His eyes narrowed and grew darker. "When I'm attracted to a woman, I don't want alcohol clouding her mind."

"Noble."

"There's that word again. I'm no hero. Just selfish."

Without anything to hold, Cassie didn't know what to do with her hands, although she'd noticed his chest was right there. In the vee of his shirt, where the top two buttons were undone, she could see a sprinkling of dark hair and the hint of muscle. Her fingers itched to explore the expanse of warm skin but, for starters, she rested one palm flat against his shirt, over his heart, which was giving a pretty good imitation of a percussion instrument.

His eyes smoldered as he gazed into her own and his breathing changed. It was subtle, but she was sure it was faster. Something had shifted in him. She'd pushed him from retreat to attack in zero point three seconds. His primal instincts were focused on her. Hadn't she always wanted to know how it would feel to have all of his attention? He was no longer ignoring her. Now what? How should she act? Active? Passive? She felt like a confused verb.

"Wh-why selfish? To make sure I'm—I mean the woman you're attracted to is sober?" she asked, feeling the need to say something.

"Because when I'm with a woman, I want her to remember me and everything I—we—do."

His voice was rough as sandpaper with a hint of smooth, warm whiskey around the edges. He was so close, his breath stirred wisps of hair around her face. The intensity of his gaze made it impossible to look away. She was mesmerized by the concentrated heat she saw in his eyes. The fire there stole the oxygen from her lungs, making her light-headed. And she felt her nerve slipping away.

Kyle had rested his palm on her bare shoulder and, with just the slightest back and forth brushing of that magic thumb, he was making her warm all over again.

She let out a long breath. "Is it hot in here?"

He shook his head. "The windows are open."

"Must be the wine. Did you know wine dilates your capillaries, increasing blood flow and circulation? In layman's terms, it warms you right up."

"All in two tiny sips? Imagine that," he said, centering his attention on her bare shoulder.

"Go figure," she said with a shrug.

He concentrated on the curve between the column of her neck and collarbone. Who knew it was an erogenous zone? It worked for her in a big way. Back and forth with his thumb. Any second she expected to see sparks, as if he was trying to start a fire by rubbing flint and steel together. Any second she expected to go up in flames. A rhythmic throbbing started between her thighs as a moist heat settled there.

What in the world was she doing?

She'd only ever been with one man, the man she'd planned to marry. She'd waited a long time for her crush on Kyle to fade. She'd been cautious and selective. Steve was the first guy to get past her defenses, the first who felt right and trustworthy. She'd given him everything: heart, body, soul and the promise of forever. What a laugh he and Lynnda must have had on her. Betrayed by her fiancé with her second-best friend in the ugliest possible way. It was one of the reasons she'd come back to California.

She'd come back all right—back to square one.

With one finger, Kyle stroked downward, over her collarbone and chest to the swell of her breast. Her breath caught as he toyed with the edge of material that covered her. Her eyelids drifted closed and her pulse hammered as she waited expectantly for him to cup her breast with his palm. One part anticipation and two parts tension coiled inside her, swirling, surging upward. She felt like a volcano about to erupt.

Then the touch was gone and she no longer felt the heat of his body in front of her. Her eyes popped open, confirming he'd taken a step back. "Wh-why did you stop?"

"I think you get the idea." His voice was hoarse and he was breathing hard.

Cassie blinked as frustration and disappointment billowed through her. It wasn't easy, but she resisted the urge to reach out and choke him.

"And your women find this satisfying?"

"They're not *my* women. And if you weren't who you are—" He ran his fingers through his hair. "Let's just say so far I haven't had any complaints."

His hand shook, she noted with satisfaction. She might be shy and somewhat inexperienced, but she would bet he wasn't as cool as he pretended. Nonetheless, he'd aborted Seduction 101. She knew from personal experience that rejection could cause permanent disfigurement of the soul. Technically this wasn't a rejection, but it was beginning to feel like one. A voice inside reminded her she was the new and improved Cassie Brightwell. She hadn't taken this risk just to roll over at the first speed bump.

But why would she want to see how far they could go? She'd been devastated by love. Only this was different from the fiancé fiasco. There was no danger of a repeat. Kyle had already warned her not to expect anything, so she had nothing to lose. He couldn't hurt her.

The last time she'd been this close to Kyle Stratton, she'd wanted desperately to know what his lips would feel like against her own. But she'd been too naive to let him know what she wanted and he hadn't taken things to the next level. A real gentleman, darn her luck.

No regrets, she reminded herself. Tomorrow, she didn't want to kick herself from here to the San Fernando Valley because she'd meekly played it his way. Especially when she had the opportunity to cancel out a big regret with a do-over. Nothing ventured, nothing gained. Damn the torpedoes, full speed ahead.

When he let out a long breath and started to back farther away, Cassie moved closer, reached up and curved her hand around his neck. Gently she urged him to lower his head, noting a startled expression in his dark eyes as she stood on tiptoe and touched her lips to his. She tasted softness, restraint, surprise and hesitation.

He lifted his mouth from hers and stared. "I thought this was my gig."

"Let me be the first to register a complaint. It seemed to me you needed a nudge in the direction I wanted to go."

"You call that a nudge? It was more like waving a red flag in front of a bull."

She smiled. "Isn't that a bit egotistical?"

"That's not what I meant. It was a metaphor for—"

"Are you blushing?"

"Of course not. Like you said, it's hot in here."

"I'm glad it's not just me." She slid her other arm around his neck and linked her fingers. "Now. You can't tell me that wimpy kiss was up to the usual Stratton standards."

"No. But that was a sneak attack. You threw me off."

She tipped her head to the side. "If you don't give me something to compare it to, I'm going to think that's the best you can do."

He settled his hands at her waist and she felt his resistance slipping. "You don't know what you're getting yourself into."

"I'm a big girl. I think I've got a pretty good idea."

"You're asking for it, Cassie." His tone held a warning, at the same time promising something that made her pulse race.

"Yes, I am."

His eyes darkened as the muscle in his jaw contracted, a visible manifestation of his internal struggle. His palms slid upward and his thumb stroked her midriff, just beneath her breast.

"Damn it," he ground out past gritted teeth as he pulled her against him. "This is a very bad idea."

Cassie sighed and closed her eyes as his mouth took hers. He nibbled tiny kisses across her lips, then with his tongue, urged her to open to him. She'd lost any will to resist the second he'd tugged her into his arms. How could she? It felt too good. But it got better when her lips parted and he delved inside her mouth, imitating the act of love. That tilted her world. If he hadn't been holding her, she would have slid bonelessly to the floor.

Then he touched the tip of his tongue to the roof of her mouth and a moan of pleasure escaped her. She knew he had heard, when his arms tightened and his breathing grew even more labored, the tension twisting inside him almost a palpable thing. Pulling his mouth from hers, he trailed kisses across her cheek and jaw, to her ear, where he took the lobe between his teeth and gently toyed with it.

It was as if an electric current shot from that point of contact, straight through her body, sensitizing every cell, every square inch of skin, every nerve ending. She couldn't seem to drag enough air into her lungs and, for the life of her, couldn't find the will to care. If she had to stop breathing, in Kyle's arms was the perfect place.

Kyle felt as if he'd just sprinted up several flights of stairs. His chest rose and fell rapidly as he tried to get more air. He pulled back and looked at Cassie.

Her cheeks were flushed, her lips swollen from his kiss, her eyes still closed in passion. She was the most beautiful sight he'd ever seen.

He wanted her any way he could get her—in his bed, on the floor, the kitchen table. It didn't matter. He wanted her more than he'd wanted any woman in his life. And he had to put an end to this before he couldn't stop himself.

He dropped his arms and dragged in air. "Enough already."

"Why?" she asked, blinking, dazed.

"We can't do this, Cassie. That kiss was a mistake."

"Your reputation was at stake."

"I don't give a damn about my reputation," he said a little too loudly. He stepped away from her as he rubbed a hand across the back of his neck.

But he did give a damn about her. Even though he had no right. Dan had said Kyle wasn't the kind of guy he wanted for Cassie. It had been true all those years ago, and every day since, Kyle had proved her brother right. If he didn't put the brakes on right now, this wouldn't be a demonstration. He would make love to her. Then there would be hell to pay.

"Kyle? What is it?" she asked, her gaze searching his face.

"I'm not hungry anymore." That was a bald-faced lie. He was hungry for her, but he could never let her know. Seeing her again, walking with her on the beach, talking to her—he'd felt an instant connection. He'd felt the emptiness inside him shrink as his need for her grew.

"I'm not sure what that means," she said.

He walked out of the kitchen to put some distance

between them. "This isn't a good idea. And I think we should call it a night."

"Okay. Maybe tomorrow we—"

"I don't think tomorrow would be any better. I need some space to think things through."

"Since when can't one friend help another friend?"

Since tonight. Since touching her had made him want to explore every single solitary inch of her skin. Since kissing her, when he'd discovered for the first time how incredibly sweet and sexy she was. Since holding her in his arms and learning she was impossible to resist. He'd barely had the strength to let her go. He knew for a fact he wouldn't be that strong a second time.

"It's just a real bad idea, Cass."

"For who?" she demanded.

"Both of us."

"I've been making decisions for myself for quite a while now. What gives you the right to call the shots for me?"

"I'm making it my right, because I'm worried about you."

"That's not your job. You're not my big brother. Dan's got that job sewn up."

Dan. Cassie had made him forget everything. Kyle had always thought of him as more than a friend, more than a brother. He'd have done anything for Dan Brightwell. In fact, he had. He'd turned his back on Cassie a long time ago. And regretted it more than once. A lot more.

"I don't want anything to get in the way of our friendship. I've lost a lot in my life, and I don't want to lose that, too."

Cassie, Dan, Megan, all the Brightwells. They were the kind of family he'd always wanted and never had. If he didn't get Cassie the hell out of there, he wouldn't be able to keep his hands off her. Everything that had ever meant anything in his life would be gone. He couldn't stand that.

He walked to the door and opened it. ''Goodbye, Cass.''

She followed him, then stopped in the doorway and glanced up. She didn't look all that different from the girl who had followed him around when they were kids. He'd known she had a crush on him. Everyone had seen it when the two families had spent summers here at the beach. They'd all thought it was cute.

It wasn't so cute now. There was a hint of hurt in her eyes. Hell, who was he kidding? He'd just sucker punched her and the pain was there staring back at him. She was damaged—again. And if she didn't stay away from him, he would keep doing the same thing over and over. Because that's the kind of guy he was. Dan had known it a long time ago.

He'd said Kyle was all flash and no substance, not the right guy for his sister. Dan had told him he could probably have Cassie, but he'd only walk away. Which was true. He had no intention of marrying, making the same mistakes his parents had. He should have turned her down flat. Instead, he'd hurt her. To-night he'd proved he was every bit the lowlife Dan Brightwell had predicted.

''Good night, Kyle. Did I thank you for the dem-onstration?'' Her voice sounded brittle, as if she might shatter into a million pieces.

''There's no need to thank me.''

''That question was rhetorical—and sarcastic.''

Then she walked across the foyer and let herself into her place, closing the door behind her. The empty blackness that had receded earlier when he'd first seen her now threatened to suck him in completely.

Cassie snuggled under the comforter and tried to ignore the ringing phone. She'd slept in her upstairs bedroom with the windows open because of the lingering paint fumes from the rooms below. The good news was she couldn't detect the odor of paint. The bad news: she was freezing. And about to go deaf from the damn phone. Apparently she was crabby, too, no doubt from a restless night thinking about Kyle, the bane of her existence.

She grabbed the receiver. "Hello?" she croaked.

"Cassie?"

"Yes."

"You sound cranky. It's Mom."

"Hi. I'm not cranky. I'm still sleeping."

She knew her mother was looking at her watch. "But it's ten-thirty, dear. Isn't this awfully late for you?"

"Rough night."

"I was starting to get worried when you didn't answer. I was about to hang up and call Kyle."

Startled, Cassie sat straight up and let the comforter pool at her waist. "Kyle? Why would you call him?"

"He's staying at his mother's place."

"How do you know?"

"Regina told me."

Thanks for the heads-up, Mom, Cassie thought. "Is that so?"

"Yes. You know we've kept in touch over the years."

Yeah, Cassie was aware of their friendship, and the way her own ears always perked up when her mother mentioned talking to his mother, hoping for news about Kyle. How pathetic was that? Especially after his brush-off exactly six days ago. She hadn't seen him since.

"Cassie, are you listening?"

"To every word, Mom," she lied. She smiled at the audible sigh on the other end that said her mother knew she was lying.

"I happened to mention to Regina that you were moving back to California for a new job and planning to spend time at the beach. She said Kyle was taking some time off to contemplate his navel—"

"Mom?"

"That was a test to see if you were listening. Also, it's sixties generation speak. Translation—he needs to do some thinking about things. Regina said she suggested he use the duplex. He agreed. Have you seen him?"

Cassie lay back down on the bed and closed her eyes. Kyle's image instantly appeared. Without a shirt. Her mouth went dry. She couldn't do anything without seeing him.

"As a matter of fact, I have seen him. We took a walk on the beach the day he got here." And she hadn't seen him since.

"That's nice, dear. How's the weather?"

"Great. You know, typical for August. It's spectacular, warm enough to stay out on the beach until sundown. After dark it gets chilly."

And dangerous. Smart girls stayed home where it was safe. Cassie wasn't so smart.

"How's Kyle?" her mother asked.

Great. Oh, and by the way, he doesn't ever want to see me again. She knew this because he was keeping a very low profile. "Kyle looks good."

And kissed good.

"He's a good-looking boy."

Boy? Not hardly. "Yeah, he is."

"Do you remember when you had a crush on him and used to follow him down to the water while he was swimming and just stand there waiting for him to notice you?"

"I didn't wait for him to notice me." With luck, her mother wouldn't notice she hadn't denied the crush part. "I was putting my feet in the water to stay cool." If only she'd stuck her foot in the water instead of her mouth that night at his place.

"Whatever you say, dear. I tried to call you last night, but you weren't in."

"Yeah. The paint fumes in here were bad, so I opened the windows and left."

"Did you go over to see Kyle?"

"Why would you jump to that conclusion, Mom?"

"I don't know." There was a shrug in her voice. "Because he's there, he's handy and you're friends."

Not anymore. But her mother didn't have to know about that. A little white lie was in order. Actually it wasn't a lie. She'd seen Kyle, just not the night before.

"I brought over steaks and salad for dinner." And got thrown out before eating anything. Hanging out with Kyle was exciting. She just didn't get to do it for very long.

"That's nice, dear. So the two of you are having a good time."

If a mind-blowing make-out session defined good

time, Cassie was having a blast. It was the part after the mind-blowing make-out session that confused the heck out of her. Oh, that was too generous. She'd been confused before she'd practically forced him to kiss her. But his reaction after that kiss had really messed up her mind. And continued to do so.

"Are you there, Cassie?"

"Yeah, Mom. Still waking up."

"There's a new coffeemaker still in its box in the pantry. But I'd rather you use the old one until the painting is finished. How's that going, by the way?"

"Good." It had given her a golden opportunity to look her worst when she'd seen Kyle again. "I have another couple days of work left. And the trim."

"Don't tire yourself out, dear."

"I won't. I'm taking it slow." There was an understatement.

"The other reason I called was to let you know the new furniture should be available for delivery in a week to ten days. Do you think you'll be finished by then?"

"Probably."

"I could send your brother up to help."

"Not on my account, although I'd love to see him. I'm sure Kyle would, too." Then the two of them could go trolling for women together. The thought made her profoundly sad and she had no idea why.

"Dan's pretty busy. His firm just snagged a very big client."

"That's great, Mom. Don't bother him, then. I'll get the painting done."

"Let me know if you fall behind."

"I will. Have you made arrangements to get rid of the old furniture?"

"No. I thought you could take care of that while you're there."

"Sure, Mom. Piece of cake." It would be a good distraction. Help her ignore the guy next door, who was so worried about her he didn't want anything to do with her.

Her mother made a noise on the other end of the line. "I just had a great idea."

"Yeah?"

"Kyle can help you dispose of the furniture."

"Oh, I don't want to bother him. I can handle it."

"Don't be shy, Cassandra. I'm sure he would be happy to help. Use him."

Cassie couldn't tell her mother she'd already tried that and she hadn't seen him since. "I'll see what I can do, Mom. But he might have other plans."

"According to his mother, he's just going to brood. You can't let him do that, dear."

Wanna bet? She didn't need to get her teeth kicked in—how many times was it now? She shook her head, deciding she didn't have the energy to count her disappointments.

"I don't want to bother him. He's got better things to do than help me." So many women, so much seduction, so little time.

"I'm sure you wouldn't be bothering him, dear. His mother said she's worried about him. I have a feeling he would welcome the distraction. If you'd like, I could call and ask for you—"

"No!"

"Cassie? Are you sure you're all right? I'm getting worried. Maybe I should call Kyle after all. Get him to pop in and have a look at you. Maybe those paint fumes are getting to you."

Cassie took several deep, calming breaths in order to decelerate her heart rate and bring her voice several octaves down to her normal range. "That's okay, Mom. I'll talk to him."

"Good. Let me know what happens. With the furniture, I mean."

"Right." What else would it be? Certainly nothing was going to happen with Kyle. "Love you, Mom. Bye."

Cassie hung up the phone and sighed. Who knew the road to hell wasn't paved with good intentions after all? It was littered with regrets.

Cassie shook her head to clear it. A pity party was no way to start out the day. She had a lot of work to do if she was going to get the painting done in time for the new furniture to be delivered.

Her bedroom was one of the Jack-and-Jill rooms with a bathroom in between. She slid out of bed and padded in to brush her teeth, then pulled her straight hair into a ponytail. After tugging on old, bleached-out cutoff sweats and a baggy T-shirt, she went downstairs.

The day before, she'd painted what she could without moving furniture out of the way. Now it was crunch time. She relocated the easy stuff first—dining room chairs, wall hangings, and emptied the dishes in the breakfront, putting them in the kitchen. The couch was an old sleeper sofa and she knew that sucker was going to be heavy. But if she could slide it away from the wall just enough…

She grabbed the arm and tried to shift it, but her fingers slipped and the momentum sent her backward, her elbow connecting with the lamp on the table behind her. It crashed to the floor and the ceramic base shattered on the unforgiving tile.

"First casualty," she muttered, feeling stupid. At least it was already slated for retirement. She started through the clutter of end tables and odds and ends in the center of the room to get the broom and dustpan. "Maybe one bad deed will cancel out the two good ones and reverse my punishment."

Kyle. Nothing could reverse that. Sighing, she shook her head.

Before she could get through the mess to the kitchen pantry, there was a knock on the door. Who could it be? She'd wished for reinforcements, but even her mother couldn't have gotten Dan there that fast.

She headed in the other direction and opened the door. It wasn't reinforcements and it wasn't Dan.

It was Kyle.

Chapter Four

"What are you doing here?"

Kyle inspected Cassie from head to toe. He'd heard the crash and feared— He didn't know what he feared, but seeing she was all right went a long way toward bringing his adrenaline level back to normal.

"I just got back from a run."

"Yeah. I figured that out." Her gaze skimmed over his damp hair, his face and settled just a little too long on his mouth before self-consciously skittering away. "Although this is a surprise."

"What?"

"I didn't expect to see you." She shrugged, drawing his attention to the oversize shirt she wore.

He knew from firsthand exploration what was under that shirt. He remembered the shape and texture of her bare shoulder, skin as smooth as silk, the flat expanse of her midriff leading to the tantalizing swell of her breast, which had nearly been his undoing that night. Was it only six days ago? It seemed longer.

After she'd left, he'd noticed her full wineglass, the lipstick mark that had been a perfect outline of her mouth. After downing the contents in one gulp, he'd brushed his thumb over that mark, yearning to kiss her again. Visions of her had tormented him most of the night. Now it took all his willpower not to grab the hem of that big shirt and skim it up, over and off her. Mostly he wanted to talk to her, see her smile and feel himself smile right back.

He was an idiot for being here. But he'd wondered about her. The last time he'd seen her, she'd looked as if she might shatter into a thousand pieces. If not for the noise he'd just heard and the growing need to know she was in one piece, he wouldn't have knocked on her door.

He shoved his fingers through his hair. "I heard something break. Something big. My ears are still ringing. I thought you might be—" He rested his hand on the door frame as he looked down at her. "Are you okay?"

She nodded. "Thanks for stopping by," she said, starting to close the door.

He easily blocked it with his palm. "Aren't you going to tell me what happened?"

"I didn't want to overstep the boundaries of friendship." She leaned her hip against the edge of the door. "After all, I just found out it's not okay for friends to hang out together. Who knew?"

She didn't understand he'd done it for her own good. He wasn't the kind of man she deserved. If their attraction got out of hand and climbed to the next level, the clock would start ticking and it was only a matter of time until everything blew up. Having her in his life and not being able to touch her was better than not seeing her at all. As he'd told her, he was a selfish bastard who was obviously into self-torment. Who knew?

"Are you going to tell me what happened or continue to act like a pouting child?"

She scrunched her face up as if she was thinking real hard about it, then she met his gaze. "I think I'll keep pouting."

"Oh, for Pete's sake, we share a common wall."

Irrelevant for this discussion, but a fact that never left his mind. She was only a few steps away, separated from him by plaster and wallboard that, more than once, he'd felt like putting his fist through. Even if he managed to doze and forget for a few brief moments, his body remembered.

"Look, Cass, I just want to make sure nothing's going to explode or catch fire." Besides me, he thought, looking at her mouth. He glanced away quickly. "I have a vested interest in this duplex. If you go down I go down. Let me make sure everything's okay. Friend to friend."

"Oh." She nodded, but the exaggerated movement did not signal acquiescence. "Thanks for clearing that up."

They stared at each other for several moments.

"Cassie." He gritted his teeth.

"Yes?" she asked sweetly.

"Are you going to let me in or not?"

"I wasn't planning on it, no."

"I could muscle my way past you."

"Why is it so important to you?" She glanced behind her. "Obviously there's no smoke or fire. Nothing's going to blow up. The duplex is safe for Mom, apple pie and—''

''The girl I left behind?''

She looked down. ''You said it. Not me.''

She was right. He'd said it because it was the truth. He *had* left her behind. Because it was the right thing to do, the best thing for her. She was also right that the building wasn't in imminent danger. But he was. He needed a reason to see her. If it hadn't been this, he would have invented another excuse, something as lame as borrowing a cup of sugar. Just to see her, talk to her. Because he'd missed her. Because she was there. If she hadn't been—

Suddenly a thought popped into his mind. She wasn't going to be at the duplex forever and neither was he. Just another week. They both had jobs to go to. The end was in sight. What could it hurt? Not a thing he could see, as long as he kept it strictly friendship. He could do that. Once before, he'd walked away from her. He could do it again.

That decided, his spirits lifted. Anticipation washed through him. But he wasn't home free yet. She hadn't agreed to stop pouting. Judging by the look on her face, there was groveling in his immediate future. For the life of him he couldn't seem to care.

''I'll give you ten seconds to change your mind,'' he said.

''Or what?'' A spark of something lit her blue eyes.

''Or I'll huff and puff and blow your house down.''

She put her hand on her hip. ''Well, that's certainly getting into character. I should have known. The big bad wolf.'' But the shadows lingering in her eyes said, *with everyone but me.*

He was sorry about that, more than she would ever

know. And he was weak. He couldn't deny himself the pleasure of her company. But that didn't mean he had to make it physical.

"I used to play football in high school," he warned. "I know how to take you down."

"Okay. Give it your best shot. We can do that cartoon thing where you get a running start then just at the right moment I open the door and you tumble into the chaos and wind up with paint all over your face."

"Or egg," he said with a sigh. "Look, Cass. I don't know what got into me the other night. I'm sorry. I want to hang out with you."

"Really?"

One corner of her mouth curved up, but he wasn't there yet. "You're not going to make this easy, are you?"

"Nope."

"That whole demonstration thing got out of hand. At the risk of stooping to the level of my inner child, you started it. I warned you. But let's forget it ever happened." Yeah, that was going to happen. "I want to be with you, friends just hanging out. Like old times. When we were kids. How do you feel about it?"

"You're not going to bury me in the sand, are you?"

He grinned and held up his hand. "Scout's honor."

"Then okay."

"But we have to set up some ground rules first."

"Such as?" she asked.

"No hanky-panky."

She stared at him for several moments, then burst out laughing. "I can't help feeling this is some kind of role reversal. Are you afraid of little ol' me?"

Yes, he wanted to say. Terrified. "Of course not." He let out a long breath. "But you've got to admit when things get to the hanky-panky level, it gets all weird and complex. Being friends with you is simple and uncomplicated. And fun. I'd like to keep it that way. What do you say?"

She opened the door wide. "I say come on in."

"Wow." He walked past her.

"Wow what?" She closed the door. "You're a lawyer. I'm agreeing with Beth Deveraux that you're the best. You made an excellent case. I'll make adequate coffee."

She wove her way through the obstacle course that was her downstairs. This unit had an identical layout to his but was the mirror image. Everything reversed albeit in chaos. Chairs were clustered in the center of the room, plastic drop cloths scattered around, cans of paint huddled together on newspapers. Rollers, pans and paintbrushes. Oh my.

He squatted down and inspected the shattered lamp on the floor beside the sleeper sofa. "Fit of temper?"

She glanced at him over her shoulder as she filled the glass coffeepot with water from the tap. "What?"

He walked to the bar, careful to keep it between them. The last time he'd seen her, she'd looked dynamite in her jeans and one-shouldered black top. But in her sweat shorts and oversize shirt, she was somehow even more appealing. And tempting.

She poured the water into the coffeemaker then measured ground beans into the filter. After flipping the switch, it took several moments for the dripping and sizzling to commence.

"Now, what did you say?"

He angled his head toward the shards of ceramic

that had once upon a time been a lamp. "How did the lamp break?"

"I was trying to move the couch away from the wall so I could paint behind it. My hand slipped and I elbowed that sucker into oblivion."

"You should have asked me for help."

"Why? Breaking it was as easy as falling off a log."

He shook his head. "I didn't mean that. You should have asked me to move the couch for you."

One delicate eyebrow rose. "Counselor, given my state of mind up until a few moments ago, do you really want to go there again?"

He laughed. "Do I have *stupid* tattooed on my forehead?"

"Let me see." She circled the bar, reached up and cupped his face in her hands, pulling him closer, as if for an inspection. As if for a kiss.

He backed away. "Very funny, Brightwell. Where's your broom? I'll clean up the glass."

"It's in the pantry."

She rested her hands on her hips, giving him a hint of the curves beneath the soft cotton of her shirt. The look on her face was cocky and challenging and cute. His undoing. As soon as she'd opened the door and he'd taken one look at her face, he knew he couldn't share a wall and not share her—unless he kept reminding himself they were just friends. If he could do that, everything would be fine.

"I just had a thought," she said.

"Uh-oh. There's a dangerous prospect. And rare," he added, grateful to be able to slip back into teasing friendship. Anything to ease the yearning ache inside him.

He walked past her and retrieved the broom, then turned back to what had once been the lamp. She continued talking as he swept.

"I'm going to ignore the dig and go to where you said you're here to evaluate your life. Is that correct?" she asked.

"It is."

"Don't you think you could do it better with a paintbrush in your hand?"

He couldn't help smiling at her cross-examination. "I don't know. My life is rules and words and books. If I need something painted, I hire a painting professional."

She snorted. "That takes all the fun out of it. If more people painted, family counselors and mental health workers would go out of business."

"Not to mention painters."

Ignoring him, she went on. "What you need to fill up your emotional well and help with your thought process is good old-fashioned manual labor."

"Maybe I don't really want to think about anything," he suggested.

"It's good for that, too. Turns your mind off."

Unfortunately, if he let that happen, she would turn his body on and send it into overdrive. Keep it light, he reminded himself. "Are you asking me to help you paint?"

"If I was, what would you say?"

If she asked him to scour the tile grout with a toothbrush, on his hands and knees, he would agree. Or clean the grease off the wheel covers on her car with a cotton swab, he would jump at the chance. As long as he could spend time with her.

"I'd say okay."

And hope like hell it wouldn't come back to bite him in the backside.

* * *

With Kyle beside her, Cassie sat on the low wall separating the sand from the sidewalk. They'd finished painting, cleaned up and walked down to the beach to watch the sunset. The evening breeze caressed her cheeks, feeling wonderful after spending the day cooped up inside working.

As the golden fireball slowly dropped behind the curve of land that jutted into the ocean, the wispy clouds in the sky turned every shade of pink, purple and yellow. She must have seen the sight a thousand times, yet every sunset was different, profound. Simply beautiful. She sighed with absolute and utter contentment.

"What was that about?" he asked, glancing at her.

"The perfect end to an excellent day." Cassie forced herself to laugh. Don't let him see she'd been dead serious, she thought. Don't spoil it. Because the whole day had been one of the best she could remember. Work had never been so much fun. Being with Kyle made everything wonderful. Painting, talking, laughing—kissing. Don't go there, she warned herself. They'd spent days apart because of kissing. Her fault. He was right about that. But, she reminded herself, don't spoil this completely flawless moment by making it mushy, or serious, or something it wasn't and never would be.

Her day had certainly started out a downer, what with the broken lamp. But even that had been a blessing in disguise.

She looked at the sky and noticed how the waning sun's golden rays swept a glow across the bottom of the clouds. "At the risk of getting into the milieu of our surroundings, have you ever thought about the saying every cloud has a silver lining?"

He followed her gaze and she heard the smile in his voice. "If you're going where I think you are, it should be golden. But what's your point? I'm sure you have one."

"Today started out so bad." She stopped short of telling him that the prospect of him being so near yet so far, of not seeing him, had dropped her spirits into the cellar. "My mother called and woke me up. I broke the lamp."

"I don't see where you're going with this whole silver-lining thing."

"Because of that broken lamp, you and I spent the day painting."

"I say again—silver lining? Painting? As in work." He held out his hands, moving them up and down as if juggling the two to see a correlation.

"It was fun. That's all. And doing it alone would have been...not fun," she finished lamely.

Brooding, he stared into the distance, at the glow above the headland where the sun used to be. "Maybe I should give up law and take up painting. Want to be my assistant? Like Holmes and Dr. Watson?"

"More like Bonnie and Clyde."

"Why?" He glanced at her. "I wouldn't be stealing anything."

Only my heart, she thought. "I was kidding," she said. "Are you so jaded you've lost your sense of humor? Even the perfection of a spectacular sunset doesn't move you?"

"It moves me, all right. And if you want to get into

milieus, there's the whole 'ocean where sharks live' thing.''

''I don't get it.''

''Lawyers are often compared to sharks.''

''You're not a shark. Yours is a perfectly fine job.''

He was back to his profession, but she couldn't help feeling it wasn't the work he wanted more from, but his personal life that was lacking.

He looked at her. ''It can be a dirty job, but I suppose someone has to do it.''

''Not true. I mean it's true that someone has to do it. But the job is nothing to be ashamed of and the pay's not bad.''

''Yeah, that makes me feel a lot better. Making a living at a job I like and I'm actually good at that sucks the life out of people. I'm doomed,'' he said, shaking his head. ''An empty shell of a man.''

''And a very nice shell it is.''

The words had popped out and Cassie wanted them back in the worst way. Let him take it lightly, she prayed. Don't let him see she'd been dead serious. Don't spoil the day. He stared at her. In the twilight, without the sun's brightness, she couldn't decipher the expression on his face. She shivered.

''You're cold. We should head back.'' He stood and held out his hand.

She took it and let him pull her to her feet. Then he quickly released her, as if her fingers were hot coals and had burned him. He stuck his hands in his pockets as they strolled back to the duplex.

''Who knew you were so shallow?'' he asked.

''Me? Shallow?''

''Yeah. That whole shell thing. Seeing only the exterior, with complete and utter disregard for my inner beauty.''

"That's me," she said. "Shallow as a sandbar. Along with the rest of the female population.''

"What does that mean?''

"It means I'm not blind. Now that I think about it," she said, "that may be part of why your well is empty. Maybe it's not your job at all. Going from woman to woman sucks the energy, if not the life, out of a person.''

He shrugged. "I haven't met anyone available who's worth putting all my energy into.''

What about me? she wanted to say. But she knew what he meant. He hadn't met anyone he was attracted to who was worth his effort. The thought made her terribly sad and she couldn't let him know.

"So for you it's all about sex?" she asked, trying to inject a happy note into her tone.

"I plead the fifth.''

"You refuse to answer on the grounds that you might incriminate yourself?''

"'Incriminate' is such an ugly word," he said, as they turned onto the walkway leading to the duplex.

"You're tap-dancing, Stratton, and you know it.''

He climbed the three steps and leaned back against one of the wide circular supports holding up the porch roof. "Are you as bored talking about me as I am?''

She could talk about him forever. "Is that your way of taking the heat off yourself?''

"No. Actually I have something else in mind for that.''

"Such as?''

"You haven't told me what happened between you and your fiancé.''

It wasn't his words but the way his tone gentled and turned tender that opened up the painful memories inside her. "You don't miss a trick, do you?"

"I'm not going to drop it. Call it a friend thing. Why did your engagement fall apart?"

"That tends to happen when you come home from work early and find your fiancé in bed with your roommate."

She was so grateful he didn't say he was sorry. She'd have been forced to sock him. Or cry. And she hadn't cried over the whole mess. She'd told herself the guy wasn't worth it. She couldn't bear it if she broke down in front of Kyle Stratton.

"I couldn't believe Lynnda would do that to me," she said. Now that the wound was open she couldn't seem to stop all the poison from oozing out. "Would you believe I asked her to share the apartment? I thought she was my friend. We worked together at the hospital. Then I introduced her to Steve. How stupid am I?"

"Not stupid at all."

"You're wrong. Sweet, but wrong. It was awfully damn dumb to let the she-devil of the planet into my home and give her access to my fiancé."

"You're not dumb—"

"Oh, yeah? It wasn't the first time I came home from work and found them together. In fact it happened a lot and he always claimed he was waiting for me. I'd get stuck at the hospital and he would ask whether I minded if he took Lynnda out to dinner. Don't you see? She stabbed me in the back and I all but handed her the knife."

"You keep saying she. What about Steve?"

"I don't know what you mean."

"He wasn't a noninterested bystander. In all likelihood he made the first move. But even if he didn't, he chose to sleep with her after asking you to marry him. He chose wrong."

She shook her head. "You don't know Lynnda. In fact, I'm not so sure she wasn't the one to suggest we share an apartment."

"Listen to me, Cass." Kyle reached for her, but she backed away. "Steve is the guy you fell in love with. I know it's easier to blame her for what happened."

But if she didn't blame Lynnda, then—oh, God. It was like all the pieces of a jigsaw puzzle falling into place, a very painful puzzle.

"You're right," she said miserably. "I didn't want to see it, but you're right. If I blame him then I really am stupid. I picked him. It was easier to believe everything was her fault, that he was too weak to resist her questionable charms than to acknowledge I chose poorly. Or worse, I wasn't enough for him." Her voice broke as a knot of emotion lodged in her throat.

Tears swam in her eyes and she was grateful the sun had set and Kyle couldn't possibly see or know. She refused to cry, especially in front of Kyle Stratton. She was fairly certain the man had never been disappointed in love. Cassie figured she was still being punished for those two good deeds. If she could spit in fate's eye, she would do it and say enough already.

"It's time for me to go in," she said, using a great deal of effort to keep her voice steady.

She opened the outside door and walked inside. With shaking hands, she fit her key into the door of her half of the duplex while he did the same on his side. She heard his door creak as it swung wide, then she pushed hers open. But she didn't hear his close. She couldn't see him but felt him standing in front of his own unit, staring at her.

"I'm sorry, Cass."

Rats. He could have gone for the rest of her life without saying those words. The last thing she wanted from him was pity. She would have her own pity party and Kyle wasn't invited. Steve hadn't wanted her. Kyle only wanted her as a friend. The sob lodged in her throat came out as a squeak. For God's sake, she couldn't even cry with grace and dignity. She cried like a mouse.

"Are you crying, Cassie?"

"No." She sniffled.

"Damn it."

"I'm not. Really."

"The hell you're not."

She hadn't heard him move, but suddenly he was there, his hands on her shoulders. He turned her into his solid, warm chest then wrapped her in his arms. She couldn't help thinking her romantic ruin had almost been worth this single shining moment.

If only she could stay there forever.

Chapter Five

Cassie knew if she had any spine at all, she would step out of his wonderful strong arms, smile like the Brightwell she was, and disappear to have her breakdown in private. She tried to pull away, but he tightened his embrace and snuggled her closer, refusing to let her go.

"Paint fumes," he explained.

God bless paint. Tears blurred her eyes as he led her over to his place. The next thing she knew, he'd flipped the switch on the wall beside the fireplace and flames appeared. Then they were sitting on the sofa and she was in his lap. She didn't know how she'd gotten there and didn't particularly care. Her teeth chattered uncontrollably and she was crying. And Kyle was there.

"You're shaking," he said, as if he needed an excuse to hold her in his arms.

"I—I never do this," she mumbled against his shoulder. "Crying on your shoulder. Literally," she said, and laughed. Or sobbed. She wasn't sure which, but there was wetness involved and she knew it was probably a sob and she wasn't a pretty sight.

"What are friends for?" His voice was husky and she could tell he was trying to keep it light.

They sat together for what could have been a few minutes or a lifetime. Cassie would never know. But finally the storm subsided. And her senses took over, making her aware of other things. Like the way Kyle's heart hammered beneath her palm. The warmth of his hands skimming over her back. Tension in his arms. Kissing her hair. His erection poking her thigh.

Her eyes widened as her breath caught. She sat up and looked at him.

"Kyle, I can't ignore that."

"Why? I can. If I can, you can. And I wish you would." His eyes smoldered as he stared at her. Then he let out a breath and said, "Oh, hell."

Taking her face between his hands, he brushed his thumb across her mouth. She shuddered as he pulled her slowly toward him. At the same time she leaned in until she was close enough for him to kiss her. He groaned as he touched his mouth to hers. Cassie felt he was holding back, as if he were struggling against himself.

She had no clue why he was conflicted, but she intended to make it as difficult as possible for him to ignore her. She slid her hands around his neck and loosely linked her fingers. Needing to be closer, she pressed against him, nestling her breasts to the muscular wall of his chest. He moaned again. Then he tightened his hands on her arms and moved her back, breaking the contact of their mouths.

She blinked. "Kyle?"

"Cassie," he said, his voice rough, like rocks tossed onto the shore by wild surf. "Look, if you're okay now, you'd better go before—"

She shook her head. "Don't. I can't stand it if you send me away."

That wasn't dramatics. She didn't think she could handle another rejection from him. The one from Steve had been bad enough. But Kyle—he'd been her benchmark for as long as she could remember, because she didn't think she would ever get this close to him. That conclusion was based on the fact he'd turned her away twice. A third time would *not* be the charm. It could destroy her.

As opposed to moving forward, being with Kyle. What could that hurt? She knew how it felt to wonder—for years to imagine—how it would feel to kiss him. She didn't want to regret not having him. It felt right. If it felt right, do it. That was her motto now. No more regrets.

She met his gaze as his hands cupped her cheeks. With his thumbs, he brushed away the lingering wetness beneath her eyes. "Cassie, I don't want to hurt you. This is…I'm not the right guy for you."

"You know—" Her voice caught and she hesitated, then met his gaze, her own skimming his tormented face. "I waited and waited for the right guy. It took me a long time—for reasons unimportant to this conversation—to be ready to take a chance on love, and look what happened. It was a complete disaster. Don't even talk to me about the right guy. There's no such thing."

"You said yourself I've got a reputation."

"I was teasing. I don't care about tomorrow."

"I do. If I hurt you—"

"You won't. I don't expect forever, just for now."

"Are you sure?"

"I've never been more sure of anything in my life. I'll go if you can tell me you don't want me."

"I wish I could," he whispered.

Kyle let out a long breath. He'd never felt more alive than he did at that moment. Cassie didn't take anything from him; she never had. She always gave freely, with all her heart. And he took. In the distant recesses of his conscience, a voice insisted he could lose everything important in his life if he didn't turn back right now. This was a mistake. Just one in a series, he thought, the worst being he'd deluded himself that he and Cassie could be just friends. The second was his arrogance, his conceit, his unshakable belief that he could turn his back on her again.

Not this time. Not after kissing her.

Not after the way she was looking at him. This time would shatter her into more pieces than the broken lamp he'd swept up that morning. He couldn't do it, to her, to himself. Damn his pesky selfish streak. He couldn't deny himself any longer.

He wrapped an arm around her waist and the other around her shoulders as he slowly lowered her to the couch. The room was lighted only by the flames from the gas log and the glow from the outside deck light streaming through the kitchen blinds. Leaning over, he studied her face. There was complete trust in her eyes. He wasn't the man to give her forever no matter how much he might want to. But he could give her for now and make it the best he knew how.

Tunneling his fingers into the silk of her hair, he leaned over her and met her trembling mouth with his own. She was soft, sweet, and tasted of sorrow and surprise. He licked her bottom lip and she opened to him, inviting him inside, a request he couldn't deny. The moist interior was warm and welcoming. As their tongues dueled and stroked, he heard her moan of pleasure. Her breathing grew hard and fast and she strained against him.

Kyle slowly unbuttoned her shirt, then pushed the edges wide, fascinated by the rapid rise and fall of her breasts. Cassie's plain white cotton bra was somehow more erotic than transparent black lace on a lingerie model. He was grateful for the front clasp, which he flicked open with two fingers. Brushing the cups aside, he looked at her, unable to believe how perfect, how beautiful she was.

"You are unbelievable," he whispered.

"Unbelievable good? Or unbelievable bad?" Her gaze was uncertain. "For a man of words like yourself, that one is not especially reassuring."

"It's actually very good." He smiled as her breath caught when he traced a finger from her collarbone down the center of her chest to her navel. "As a man of words, I'm here to tell you 'unbelievable' means you're so beautiful there aren't any words special enough for you."

Her full lips curved upward. "Good save."

"That wasn't a line. It's the absolute truth." He traced the swell of her breast with his finger, brushing it across her rosy nipple, which instantly snapped to attention.

She seemed to relax, in spite of the obvious sexual tension. But she wasn't hesitant or shy with him.

Maybe because they knew each other so well. He shook his head. It was more than that. It was as if, after wishing for something, her dream had finally come true and she embraced the moment.

He touched her other nipple and smiled when it had the same reaction as the first. "There's another truth about you. You're sensitive and passionate and so beautiful it hurts."

"Silver-tongued devil." The words were teasing, but the fire's glow caught the sheen of tears in her eyes.

"Silver tongue? As you wish."

Gently he cupped her breast, holding her ready as he took the tip in his mouth. Her gasp of delight made him smile as he laved the peak with his tongue. She squirmed in his arms as the pleasure spread through her, driving her crazy. He wanted to drive her wild, make her want him as much as he wanted her.

Apparently it worked because she slid her hands down his chest and went to town on his buttons. When she had them all undone, she tried to brush the shirt off his shoulders but it hung up on his arms. He quickly shrugged out of it.

"Turnabout is fair play," she teased.

Her talk wasn't cheap, he realized. With one finger, she teased his nipple, which instantly went taut. The touch was like an electric shock arcing pleasure to every nerve ending in his body. She put both palms on his chest, then closed her eyes, smiling as if she was savoring the feel of him.

"You have just the right amount of hair on your chest," she said.

"So do you."

Her eyes popped open. "I do not!"

"Just checking to see if you were paying attention." He grinned. "You're completely perfect."

"No." She shook her head and lifted her hand, sticking out her pinkie. "See this scar? It's from when I was six and stuck my finger in the hinge part of the door and dared Dan to shut it."

"And he did." He winced. "I remember. You sat next to me in the ER waiting to have the tip reattached."

Kyle took her wrist and brought her hand close to his mouth. He traced the scar with his tongue then took the finger into his mouth and sucked. Her moan of desire was music to his ears.

"Way to replace a bad memory with a good one," she whispered, her voice husky, sexy. "Remember that Fourth of July? I know you were there, and Dan and Megan and Amy. Someone threw a sparkler and it caught me on the back of the leg?"

"Yeah, I remember." That one had been worse than the finger.

"I could use more replacement therapy."

"You don't think it's dangerous hanging out with me?"

"Not if you kiss all my boo-boos that way."

He looked at her, desire brimming in her eyes. She moved sinuously, like a contented cat. "No more boo-boos. Not if I can help it. Only good memories."

He snapped open the button on her denim shorts, lowered the zipper and kissed her abdomen, satisfied when she sucked in a breath. Without removing her clothing, he slid his hand inside the waistband of her panties, then moved lower until he felt her curls and the moist warmth between her thighs that signaled she was ready for him.

With one finger, he entered her and searched until he found the nub he was looking for. He grinned when that got her undivided attention. Her body stilled in anticipation and he rubbed back and forth until her hips moved, matching his rhythm and pressing herself against his hand. She was breathing harder, faster. Attack, retreat, advance. Over and over he brushed her point of pleasure until she cried out his name. Her heavy-lidded expression and the way she gripped his forearm told him she'd shattered, in a very good way. A good memory.

She opened her eyes wide. "That was amazing." Raising herself on her elbows, she said, "Now it's your turn."

"There's a problem."

She blinked. "Don't even try to tell me you have a war injury. I know for a fact that's not true."

He laughed and shook his head, then let out a long breath. Raking his fingers through his hair, he said, "Not even close. I want you right now more than anything. I want to be inside you."

"But?" she asked, confusion casting a shadow in her eyes.

"I don't have a condom." He never made that mistake. He'd told her children weren't in his plans. But the bottom line was that he would cut off his right arm before hurting her like that.

"What?" She shook her head. "I'd believe a war injury before an excuse like that."

"It's not an excuse. I came here to be alone and think things through. Not to—"

"What kind of a Boy Scout are you?"

"What's that got to do with anything?"

"Always be prepared."

"Ah. Is this a bad time to confess I never joined the Scouts?"

"No kidding." She groaned and flopped backward, her legs across his thighs, the back of her hand over her eyes. "I thought this summer house was seduction central. Between you and Dan—"

She dropped her arm and sat up. "Wait. I think I've got it."

"What?"

Cassie wasn't ready for this to be over. Mostly she didn't want it to end like this. She wasn't going to let a little thing like a condom keep her from having the most phenomenal, wonderful night of her life. Instead of being nervous, she was completely at ease with Kyle. It was as if they were two halves of a whole. And she wanted to be whole with him in every sense of the word.

She wouldn't let anything spoil this experience she'd waited so long for. And she wanted to do everything in her power to make it extraordinary for Kyle, too. Part of not having regrets was doing your best.

"Cassie? What have you got?"

She sighed at the spectacular view of his chest, then swung her legs off his. Tipping her face up for his kiss, she said, against his lips, "Wait here. If you know what's good for you, you won't move from this spot."

"I don't think I could move if I wanted to," he answered, his voice the tiniest bit strangled.

Zipping up her shorts, Cassie turned and raced from the room, across the foyer and into her side of the duplex which, fortunately, she'd left unlocked. Taking the stairs two at a time, she went into Dan's bedroom and yanked open the nightstand drawer. Scattered inside were magazines, books and scraps of paper.

Frantically she rummaged through the mess, her fingers scraping the bottom of the drawer. She felt something and shoved stuff aside to pull out a foil packet. She held it up and kissed it.

"Hallelujah," she said, and started from the room. Glancing uncertainly over her shoulder, she went back and rooted around until she found several more. "You never know," she whispered, grabbing a handful.

Turning, she retraced her steps back to where she'd left Kyle, praying her window of opportunity hadn't slammed shut. True to his word, he still sat there.

"What kept you? I could have read *War and Peace.*"

She held the squares up as if they were five cards in a royal flush. "Pay dirt. And I wasn't gone that long."

There was a frown in his eyes. "Where did you find those?"

She sensed confessing it would spoil the moment and simply said, "You don't want to know."

"Okay." He took them from her and smiled.

Now what? Standing in front of him, she clutched the sides of her shirt together, her unclasped bra bunching uncomfortably underneath.

He stood up and cupped her face in his palms. Lowering his mouth to hers, he kissed her with the promise of renewed passion, making her heart soar.

"Let's go upstairs. I want this to be special, not just a quickie on the couch."

"Okay."

Hand in hand they mounted the stairs. Kyle flipped a switch and illuminated the hall light. They turned to the left, passing the Jack-and-Jill bedrooms with the bath in between. He led her into the master suite, stopping beside the king-size bed covered by a quilt with seashells and sea horses. He dropped her hand to fold down the comforter, blanket and sheet. Then he turned to her, the uncertainty in his expression visible in the light from the hall.

"Are you sure, Cassie?"

She nodded. "Very."

He reached out and tugged her to him, then turned her so that she was between him and the bed. Nudging his fingertips beneath her bra straps, he slipped it, along with her shirt, from her shoulders and let the whole tangled mess slide to the floor in a heap. She did the same to him, minus the bra. He pulled her against him, groaning as her naked breasts pressed to the bare, hard wall of his chest.

"That feels like heaven," he said. The words were hardly more than a breath of air spoken into her hair.

She knew what he meant. Skin to skin, no barriers between them, she loved the feel of him. He kissed her gently, then nibbled caresses across her chin, her jaw, and lower to her neck. With little effort, he found a spot that made her want to shout hallelujah again. Her body flooded with feeling—tension, expectation, exhilaration—at the contact. Her heart pounded, kicking up her pulse and respirations, not to mention speeding blood flow from head to toe.

Then he slid his hands to her waist. After unfastening her shorts, he pushed all her clothing off her hips and down her legs, letting her step out of them. Her fantasy of making Kyle regret ignoring her had always ended with his jaw dropping when he saw her in the little black dress. She'd never entertained the possibility of his jaw dropping when he saw her naked. She hoped it would drop—in a good way.

He reached out and cupped one breast, his eyes telling her that he liked what he saw as he brushed his thumb over the peak. The expression of awe, reverence, approval on his face gave her courage and made her bold. She reached out and unbuttoned his shorts. He slowly pushed them down along with his briefs, letting his erection spring free.

Then he lifted her in his arms and the romantic gesture melted her insides like butter in a hot pan. It was so tender and sweet and irresistible. She put her arms around his neck and clung to him as he braced onc knee on the bed, then set her gently in the middle, stretching out beside her on the cool sheets. His body was strong, his skin warm against her own as he snuggled her against him.

He took her mouth in a kiss that started sweet but turned wild as his palm cupped her between her legs. When he inserted one finger, she was moist and ready. For him. She felt as if she'd waited all her life for this moment and couldn't be more ready. Reaching over, he took one of the foil packets he'd dropped onto the nightstand. He held one corner, then ripped it open with his teeth. He put it over the tip of his erection and struggled to roll it down one-handed.

Cassie tentatively reached out and helped him cover himself, reveling in the sensation of soft skin over steel. Her chest felt tight and her breath caught in her throat. He was all taut muscle and aroused male. He was strong and sleek and so handsome. The sight of him was burned in her mind forever. But she wanted more. She wanted to feel. She wanted him inside her—now.

Somehow he must have known, because in one fluid motion he was kneeling between her legs, his erection nudging the apex of her thighs. When she extended her hand and closed her fingers around the hard length of him to guide him home, he groaned in pleasure. The sound made her smile even as it became more difficult to draw breath into her lungs.

He entered her in one powerful motion and she gloried in the way her body stretched to accommodate him. He braced his hands on either side of her head, most of his weight on his forearms to keep from crushing her. Slowly he entered and retreated. Over and over he repeated the movement, subtly picking up speed, his face a mask of concentration. Sweat beaded on his forehead as he thrust into her, spiking her desire, intensifying her pleasure. Tension grew in the center of her being until she couldn't hold it back. Finally she fractured into a thousand bright crystals, floating, free-falling.

Before she grew whole again, she felt one final thrust and he groaned. She heard the sound, as if it came from somewhere deep inside him, from the very depths of his soul. A profound, bottomless reverberation of intense gratification. Then the muscles bunched in his arms as he went still. She felt the shock waves that cascaded through him and smiled with supreme female satisfaction. Real life was so much better than fantasy, and naked beat the little black dress all to hell.

He rolled off her and instantly she missed the warmth of his body. He disappeared into the bathroom for several moments, then she felt the bed dip from his weight when he slid in beside her again. He slipped his arm beneath her and nestled her against him. She was grateful he'd taken the initiative, because that was exactly where she wanted to be. She felt completely boneless, as if she could never move on her own again. Except for the smile that curved her lips.

"I'm going to take a wild guess and say that's the look of a satisfied woman." His voice held traces of passion mixed with amusement.

"You'd be correct."

"Would I also be correct in assuming you're no longer upset about Steve?"

"Steve who?"

"I guess I kissed that boo-boo goodbye."

"And good riddance," she said sleepily.

Snatches of a song drifted through her mind. Something about tomorrow. If it never came. About saying I love you.

She almost wished tomorrow wouldn't come. She wished she could freeze this moment in time. She didn't want to think about anything, analyze what had happened. What if it meant more than just washing away regrets?

She was afraid it meant more than she could bear.

Chapter Six

Kyle grabbed his sunglasses and the latest *New York Times* action-thriller bestseller, then headed outside to the deck beyond the kitchen. Taking a deep breath, he dragged in a healthy helping of fresh, salty sea air. The sky was blue, there was a slight breeze and the temperature was about seventy-two degrees. The day couldn't have been more perfect. Life didn't get any better than this.

He glanced to his right, at the Brightwell half of the patio, separated from his by a wooden railing. Then he thought about Cassie, the fact that she wasn't there and his good mood slid down the tubes quicker than an egg from a Teflon pan.

Damn it.

After a night of the best sex he'd ever had in his life, he should have felt like a million bucks. Instead, he felt restless, irritable, unsettled. Normally this was when he began the mental process of letting a woman down easy. If he didn't, inevitably talk turned to a house, white picket fence and kids. Cassie was right. Going from woman to woman did suck the energy out of him. But what else could he do? The woman he wanted was off-limits.

He sat on the chaise lounge and opened the book. After reading the first few pages, he realized he hadn't a clue what he'd just read. Instead of the words, all he saw was Cassie's face.

God, he missed her.

Running his hands through his hair, he let out a long breath. Pride goeth before a fall had never been more true. In spite of their newly discovered intimacy, he'd been sure he would have the strength to turn away from her when the time came. He'd been so certain he played the game better than her. But he hadn't counted on the fact that the game had different rules when he was playing with Cassie.

Instead of finding a way to walk away, he couldn't wait to see her again. She'd fallen asleep in his arms. During the night, they'd awakened and made love several more times. He grinned, remembering her with the assortment of condoms in her hand. Later he'd been grateful.

This morning she'd bounced out of bed and said she had errands to do. A pre-employment physical and paperwork for the job she was starting in a week. She'd made arrangements for her furniture to be delivered to her new apartment. He wasn't sure she wasn't making her own excuses to walk away, because she regretted making love with him. All the things she'd said she was doing signaled an end—to him, her and this idyllic interlude. The thought hit his gut and sank like a stone.

As long as he lived, he would remember this time with her as the best he'd ever had. Having her in his bed last night was the icing on the cake and he would never forgive himself if she was somehow hurt because of it.

Kyle knew he was in a lot of trouble. He should be grateful for this reprieve, this separation to distance himself from her so he could find the strength to leave her.

Because he didn't delude himself into believing there was a snowball's chance in hell of them having a successful relationship. Not having kids was a deal breaker for her. But he couldn't be the guy who fathered her children. He didn't know how to be a good father, and Cassie deserved someone who could give her the house with the white picket fence and the kids to go along with it.

Then there was Dan and his reaction to the two of them as a couple. What would he say if he found out not only had Kyle ignored his prime directive not to see Cassie, but he'd slept with her, too. Not his finest hour, although it damn well felt like the finest hour he'd ever known.

"Hi, Uncle Kyle."

He looked to his right and saw Bayleigh Brightwell, Cassie's five-year-old niece, resting her arms on the railing. He'd been so wrapped up in his thoughts, he hadn't heard her come out.

"Hi, Bayleigh."

"Watcha' doin'?"

"Reading."

"It doesn't look like it."

"No?"

She shook her head, her straight silver-blond hair swaying with the movement. With one finger, she nudged her wire-rimmed glasses up more securely on her nose. She looked like a miniature adult.

"You weren't even looking at the pages. Your book is closed."

"So it is," he said, glancing at it in his lap. "I guess I was just thinking."

"It didn't look like thinking. You had a funny look on your face. Like you had a tummy ache."

"I did?" Perceptive kid, he thought. This complicated mess with Cass felt a lot like a tummy ache. "Trust me. I was thinking."

"'Bout what?"

"Stuff."

"What stuff?"

Your Aunt Cassie's body, her eyes, her smile, the captivating way she has of making things better just by being there. About the fact he hated that she wasn't there. About how hard it was going to be to survive after he let her go. None of which he could tell this child, so he decided to change the subject.

"Did you hitchhike to Carpinteria?"

"What's that?" she asked, wrinkling her cute little freckled nose, which was hardly big enough to support her glasses.

"It's when you stand by the side of the road, hold out your thumb like this," he said, and cocked his own in demonstration, "and hope someone will stop and give you a ride to where you want to go."

She gave him a pitying look. "I'm only five, Uncle Kyle. Mommy says I'm not supposed to go out alone.

She says not to talk to strangers. And never, ever get in a car with someone I don't know.''

"Your mom is a very smart lady.''

"Thank you very much.''

Megan Brightwell joined her daughter on the deck. She was about two years younger than Cassie, the same age as his sister Amy. The two of them used to hang out together when they all spent summers here at the beach. He and Dan, Megan and Amy. Cassie the forgotten middle child.

Things had sure gotten complicated when they grew up. Megan had fallen in love, gotten pregnant. Bayleigh had been born, developed vision problems and her father had disappeared, leaving her and Megan in the lurch. The miracle of a cornea transplant had restored the little girl's sight, but he had a feeling it would take more than a miracle to restore Megan's faith in men.

He looked at the woman who so resembled Cassie, leaning on the railing next to her daughter. "I guess the fact that you're here means Bayleigh didn't hitchhike,'' he said.

Megan laughed. "Not in this lifetime. Cassie invited us up a week ago. I'm between assignments with the home-health-care company and the ER doesn't have me scheduled for a per diem shift for a couple days.''

At least Cassie wasn't using her sister as a shield so she wouldn't be alone with him, he thought. The idea annoyed the hell out of him. He was wrestling with a future minus Cassie at the same time he didn't want to distance himself from her.

"And Bayleigh will be starting kindergarten soon.''

"No kidding? It seems like she was just born."

"Tell me about it. But this is the summer swan song. The last hurrah before the big time. And it seemed important to Cassie that we come up and spend some time with her." She grinned. "Just between you and me, I think she's planning to put us to work."

"Doing what?"

"Painting. I thought she'd have it finished up by now. The furniture needs to be gone in a couple days so they can bring in the new stuff. I can't imagine what Cassie's been doing all this time."

He didn't have to imagine, and the thought of everything they'd done together made him hard. "So you and Bayleigh are reinforcements?"

She nodded. "But with weather like this, who wants to be indoors? Or go to school," she said, looking with undisguised adoration at her daughter, who had wandered away and was now tugging sand toys out of a plastic basket by the back door.

He met her gaze. "Yeah, I hear that. I used to hate this time of year. The thought of going back to school—" He shook his head.

"I thought you loved it. You were a good student. Being star quarterback of the football team was the only thing that spared you the label 'brainer geek.'"

"I got good grades."

For good reason and not because he was a brainer. He'd buried himself in studies and sports to take the edge off his home life. It always suffered by comparison after a summer at the beach house ended. It was the only time he had the family he always craved. He wondered if Megan, Dan and Cassie knew how lucky they were to have their parents and each other.

When Kyle went back to the real world, his reality was all about stepdads or his mother's latest fling, depending on where she was in her romantic cycle. Visitations, child custody, alimony and child support. Anger, resentment, retaliation, push-pull.

He and Amy were like pawns in a tug-of-war. He still remembered feeling as if the world was coming to an end when it came out that they didn't have the same father, even though their parents were still married when his sister was born. After the truth of their mother's affair hit the fan, the marriage was over. He and his sister were like ships passing in the night. Poor Amy. She was as mixed up as he was. Maybe more.

"Earth to Kyle."

"Hmm?" he said, glancing at Megan.

"Bayleigh's right. You do look like you've got a tummy ache. Anything you'd care to discuss?"

"Not unless your nurse's training turned up a treatment for dysfunctional families."

"If so, I'd have a dad for Bayleigh."

"At least you're not alone."

She looked at her daughter again. "Yeah. In spite of all the medical problems, the worry, the fear of not having what it takes to raise a blind child if we hadn't found a donor for the cornea transplant, I wouldn't trade the experience of being Bayleigh's mom for anything in the world."

"So you worry about being good enough?"

She laughed. "No. I know I'll never be good enough for her. I just do the best I can for her every day. Sometimes my best is better than other days, but it's all I've got. And I just keep on keeping on. One foot in front of the other."

"She's a lucky little girl."

Because even though Megan was a single parent, she'd learned how to do it right from her own mom and dad. They'd always been there for her, their other two kids and each other. She had positive role models. He'd had the Bickersons. The Brightwells had been married for over thirty years. His family was revolving doors, musical chairs—mix and match.

"It doesn't feel lucky from where I'm standing," Megan said with a sigh. "I wish I could give her what I had growing up—a stable, two-parent home."

"You should have let me go after him. Legally. If nothing else, he should be paying support."

She shook her head. "If he didn't want to stay voluntarily, I didn't want money. But I'm grateful that you got him to sign off any future claim to custody."

"I just wish there was more I could do."

She smiled. "You know, things would have been so much simpler if I'd fallen in love with you. You're exactly the kind of man I'd want for Bayleigh's father."

She was so wrong, he thought. But he wasn't willing to go there. "You'll meet someone."

"If I don't, will you be a stand-in dad?"

He laughed but, even to himself, it sounded just this side of bitter. "I thought you loved your daughter."

"I do."

"Then you wouldn't want to stick her with me, even as a substitute. Don't worry. Mr. Right will come along."

"Mr. Right?" She scoffed. "Who died and made you the romance police? And how would you know anything about falling in love? I thought you and Dan were die-hard, dyed-in-the-wool playboy bachelors. Although Bayleigh thinks you're better than Beach Blanket Barbie. You should have kids—"

"Do you know where Cassie is?" he interrupted. "Have you spoken to her today?"

"For a smooth operator, that was a very unsmooth move," she said. "If you don't want to talk about it, all you had to do was say so."

"Okay. I don't want to talk about it."

"Okay. Cass should be here soon. I ran into her at Mom's house and she was right behind me. At least I thought she was. I'll call Mom. I need to talk to her anyway. She needs a status report on the duplex in case she wants to call in qualified painting reinforcements. Later, Kyle."

"See you. And, Megan?" When she turned back, he said, "Let me know when your sister gets here." She nodded and went inside.

He had no reason or right to worry or be concerned about Cassie. But that didn't alter the fact that he did and he was. It was ridiculous, irrational, and just plain stupid. But he couldn't help himself. And that worried him almost as much, because even a romantically challenged man like him was pretty sure that irrational concern was a prerequisite to being in love with someone.

Cassie and Megan sat in matching beach chairs on the sand. It was heading toward early evening and there wasn't a lot of sunlight left. A cooling breeze blew onshore, brushing the hair back from her face. They watched Bayleigh just a short distance away, playing in the wet sand by the water with a bucket and shovel.

"So did you see Kyle after you got here?" Megan asked, absently flipping through the magazine in her lap.

"No." She felt Megan's gaze on her.

"I think he's worried about you."

"I'm fine."

"I know that, but he doesn't."

"It's not his day to watch me," Cassie said with a shrug.

Megan closed the magazine and set it aside. "What's going on with you two?"

"Nothing."

"Uh-oh."

Cassie turned and looked at her sister. "What does that mean?"

"You said that in the exact same tone as when you were sixteen and Dan teased you about having a crush on Kyle. You were the queen of denial then and you're working on empress status now. You're in love with him."

"No." She shook her head and hoped her tone had matured since her lovelorn days. She wasn't stupid. She was an intelligent health-care professional who learned from her mistakes. She refused to be in love with Kyle Stratton.

"No? That's all you have to say?"

"It's enough. If I say more, you'll just accuse me of protesting too much."

"You know me too well." Megan glanced to her right. "Speaking of the devil—"

Cassie followed her sister's gaze and saw Kyle walking through the sand toward them. The words had never been more true. He was handsome as the devil and she was in emotional hell because of him, damned if she fell in love with him, which she was well on her way to doing.

He was wearing tan cotton shorts and a snug, black T-shirt that hugged his torso and outlined the muscles in his chest and arms. His legs were strong and tanned, with a dusting of masculine hair. As she watched him move closer, she didn't miss the fact that female heads turned to look at him. He broke hearts wherever he went.

Including hers—for the second time. The patch job she'd done on it sure hadn't held. She cared a lot about him, and the last thing he wanted was a lasting relationship that included home, hearth and offspring.

"Hello, ladies. May I join you?"

"Sure." Megan stood. "Take my chair. I promised Bayleigh I'd play with her."

Cassie could have cheerfully throttled her sister. This wasn't a good time to leave her alone with Kyle. But then, no time was good.

"Thanks, Megan." Kyle lowered his luscious, lanky frame into the low chair her sister had vacated.

In silence, they watched Megan join her daughter at the water's edge.

"So," he said, "did you get all your errands taken care of?"

"Yes." She held out her arm with the bandage in the bend of her elbow. "Physical's done and I've got the battle scar to prove they took blood."

"How about your apartment?"

"Everything went off without a hitch. Like clockwork. Couldn't have gone better. Furniture and boxes arrived right on schedule within the time frame the movers gave me."

"Good. I'm glad."

She glanced at him, at the brooding expression on his face. She knew she was going to kick herself for asking, but— "You don't sound glad. Something wrong?"

"Did Megan mention that I wanted to know when you got back?"

"Don't tell me you missed me." Say yes, she thought. She didn't want to be the only one.

"I wondered, when Megan said you were right behind her after leaving your mom's."

"Oh." Too much to hope he'd been as lonely for her as she'd been for him. "I was on my way out the door and Mom called me back. She remembered she had some mail for me. We got to talking, you know how it is."

"Not really. What with my whacked-out upbringing and all." He watched a seagull glide on a current of air. "I asked Megan to let me know—"

"We got sidetracked. Bayleigh was in a hurry to come to the beach. Were you worried about me, Stratton?"

"Of course not. But stuff happens. And we're friends."

Friends? Friends! Who was he kidding? After sleeping together the night before, they'd crossed over into something besides friendship, something she really and truly didn't want to name. Did he regret making love to her? Is that why he was backpedaling into the whole friends thing?

She could never be sorry for what had happened. It was the best night of her life. That didn't mean it was okay for it to happen again.

But it was hard not to want that when he was sitting inches away. She could feel the heat from his skin where their forearms rested on their side-by-side chairs. She could smell the fragrance of his cologne mixed with suntan lotion and tangy sea air. The result was tantalizing, irresistible. Which was why Megan shouldn't have left them alone.

Now that she'd experienced the wonder of being with Kyle, she knew how hard it would be to stop herself from doing it again.

But she'd learned something from their time together. There was a good reason she'd found her fiancé sleeping with her roommate. The signs had been obvious and Cassie had ignored them all, moved forward as if everything was hunky-dory. Her acute attraction to Kyle showed her she was the wrong woman for Steve and he was the wrong man for her.

Cassie now knew the right man, the only man. The thought brought a stab of pain that drove the air from her lungs. If she thought there was hope, she would try. But what was the point? He'd flat out told her he wasn't a marrying kind of man who wanted children. Anything less would break her heart in the long run. She'd known the end before there had even been a beginning. Another night in Kyle's arms would be ignoring the problem and a huge mistake.

"Yeah, friends," she said.

"Cass? You look like you've got a tummy ache."

She turned and met his gaze. "What?"

A smile turned up the corners of his mouth. "Bayleigh said that to me earlier. Before you got back. I was on the patio reading. Or trying to."

"You couldn't?"

He shook his head. "I was thinking about you."

"And that's what made you look sick?"

"The terminology was Bayleigh's, not mine. You need to take into consideration she's only five."

"I see. So you looked sick."

"I probably looked concerned."

"Not worried?"

"Nah. Definitely concerned. You left in a hurry this morning."

"I'd forgotten all about my employment physical and I was late. I hate being late. It's at least an hour drive to Valley General without traffic."

"I know. That's what you said. But I was—"

"Concerned?"

"Yeah. I didn't want you to be sorry about last night."

"What made you think I was sorry?"

He shrugged. "Just a feeling. That you might be avoiding me."

"Silly you," she said, wondering when he'd gotten so perceptive. "Why would I regret last night?"

He picked up her sister's magazine and rolled it into a tube that he slapped into the palm of his hand. "You've mentioned my reputation a time or two. I just didn't want you to think last night had anything to do with that."

"The whole playboy thing."

"Right. That you were a notch on the bedpost."

"I didn't think that." Only because it hadn't crossed her mind yet. Someday she would have to thank him for bringing it up.

"I just thought you should know it meant a lot to me."

"Me, too. I'll never forget it." What an understatement that was. The details of Kyle loving her replayed like a video, as if they were branded on her brain. And would be forever.

"I've enjoyed hanging out with you," he said.

"Yeah. It's been fun."

"It's good to see Megan and Bayleigh. We should have a barbecue on the patio tonight."

"That's a great idea."

"How long is she staying?"

"A few days. She offered to help me find a place to take the old furniture. Out with the old, in with the new."

"I could help with that."

"Okay. And between the three of us, the painting should be finished up in a day, maybe two."

"It will be our swan song."

"What?"

"Just something Megan and I were talking about. The end of—summer."

"Okay. All swans assemble 0200 hours."

Cassie struggled for cheerfulness. Her time with Kyle was almost over. Technically, with her niece and sister visiting, it was already kaput. She'd invited them when she thought Kyle would stick to his guns about not hanging out together. It was all her fault. A regret, damn it. So much for the promise to herself. She sighed. Probably this was for the best.

When he went his way and she went hers, maybe it wouldn't hurt quite so much. Yeah, as if she was that lucky after those two good deeds she was still being punished for.

Chapter Seven

Kyle strolled State Street in Santa Barbara with Cassie beside him and couldn't help feeling life was good. Especially when he'd accidentally brush her arm because they were walking too close. Her flesh was warm and soft and reminded him of how good she looked naked. That snug yellow T-shirt and her khaki shorts revealed her slender, shapely legs but still hid far too much skin as far as he was concerned.

Either he was in heaven, or on his way to hell in a handbasket. For a man who should be preparing to say goodbye, he was having far too many thoughts that would take him in the opposite direction.

They had just finished lunch at a little café in Paseo Nuevo with outside tables scattered over the red-tiled patio. The weather was perfect, the sun shining in a clear blue sky, just enough breeze to keep it from being hot. The mountains looked close enough to reach out and touch. Cassie *was* close enough, a thought that made him wish they were somewhere less public. So it was probably for the best they had left the duplex and embarked on this excursion to find a donation location for the old furniture from the Brightwell side.

Megan had left that morning. She'd spent one night with Cassie and decided to go home because her daughter began to run a temperature.

"It's too bad your sister had to leave earlier than she'd planned," he said, trying to sound sincere. He wasn't sorry to be alone with Cassie, but he sincerely felt bad that Megan's little girl was listless and not her usual chatterbox self. "I hope Bayleigh's fever turns out to be nothing."

"Yeah. She's one of those kids you're always going to worry about. Because of her medical history, every sneeze is a concern." Cassie looked up at him as they continued to stroll. "But since Megan and I are health-care professionals, I told her we could take care of Bayleigh here just as well as she could at home. This is Santa Barbara, not the wilds of Kaz-something-stan, but my sister insisted on being closer to her own doctor."

"I can understand that."

"You can?"

"Sure. If she was my kid, I'd want to play it safe."

"Yeah. If she was my kid, I would probably do the same thing," she agreed. She glanced up at him again and smiled. "She likes you."

"Megan? I like her, too."

"I meant Bayleigh, and you know it. You're pretty good with her."

Kyle recalled Megan saying he was the kind of

man she wanted for Bayleigh's father. He wanted to believe she was right, but he was a long shot. Then he met Cassie's gaze and shook his head. "This is where I change the subject. It's too bad your sister didn't get a chance to lend a hand with the painting."

"There's not that much left, although I know she felt bad about not being able to help." She shrugged. "I'll get it done by the time the new furniture arrives. I work best under pressure of a deadline."

"Speaking of pressure," he said, looking up and down the street, trying to ignore the tension he still felt from wanting her. "I thought that thrift shop your sister mentioned was around here somewhere."

"Explicit directions are not my sister's strength. An address or a name would have been way too helpful." Cassie stopped walking and shielded her eyes from the sun. She pointed to a store across the street. "I don't know if that's the place Megan was talking about, but it looks interesting."

"Okay."

He tugged her along to the signal light and waited for it to turn green, then crossed the palm-tree-lined street. Backtracking, they found the store called Everything Old...Is New Again. The display window was littered with lamps, vases, pictures, a small writing desk and cedar chest, along with all kinds of odds and ends. A notice on the door read, "The management gratefully accepts items for the Santa Barbara Women's Shelter. Everything must be in good condition. Pickup service available upon request. All donations are tax deductible."

"This could work," he said, pointing at the sign.

"Let's check it out," she agreed.

As he opened the door and let Cassie precede him,

he couldn't shake the feeling that the store's name had hit a nerve with him. Everything old is new again. He and Cassie were old friends, but he'd discovered feelings for her that were different and new and unsettling, but boy were they exciting.

The interior of the store was dark after the bright sunlight. He removed his sunglasses and hung them from the neck of his T-shirt. It took several moments for his eyes to adjust. The wooden floor didn't help lighten the inside. Neither did the clutter; there was stuff everywhere. Glassware, tableware, knickknacks, quilts, occasional tables, kitchen appliances, pots and pans. The jumble was stacked so high, no way could light get into this place.

Behind the counter, a woman looked to be totaling sales receipts. She was attractive, somewhere in her mid to late thirties with brown hair and green eyes.

"Hi," she said, looking up to meet his gaze. "If there's anything I can do for you, let me know."

"Do you mind if we browse?" Cassie asked.

"Help yourselves."

When she smiled, Kyle noticed a scar on her upper lip and figured she had a story. He wasn't especially intuitive, but he'd read the notice in the window. It didn't take a mental giant to figure she had a personal interest in the women's shelter. He'd handled a couple cases for wives leaving abusive relationships. If the husband had approached him, he'd have refused the case. After all, he had his standards. There was no reason, ever, for a man to hit a woman.

Cassie picked up an oval plate. "This looks old. My mom collects green Depression glass. I wonder if it's from that era. Do you think she'd like it?"

He moved behind her, taking advantage of the

close quarters to get near enough to brush against her and feel her shiver. He leaned over her to look. "It's nice."

"Nice?" She glanced up at him over her shoulder. "Look at the detail in the pattern, the flowers and leaves. At the very least it rates a heartfelt *really* before that generic *nice*."

"Okay."

She picked up the price tag and looked at the hand-written figure. "Not too bad. I'm going to buy this."

"What if it's not authentic?"

"Someone once told me if you like something and it brings you pleasure, it doesn't matter whether it's the real McCoy or not."

"It's for a good cause."

"Yeah. I think this is the place Megan was talking about."

"While you poke around in here, I'll negotiate with the woman up front about taking the furniture," he offered.

"Negotiate? Can't you just talk to her?"

He grinned. "Okay."

"Thanks."

Kyle retraced his steps and stopped at the glass counter where the woman was still going through receipts.

"Yes?" she said.

"My...friend has a duplex south of here in Carpinteria," he started.

"I know it. Nice little town," she said.

"Her mother is having new furniture delivered in a few days. The old pieces are in good shape, but—"

"It's time for a change?"

"Yeah. Do you take stuff like that?"

She nodded. "It's exactly what we need, whatever makes a home. Anything you need to be comfortable, we need at the shelter. We'd be happy to take it off your hands."

"Great. How do we do this?"

"Can you give me a detailed list? I have a truck and volunteers to pick it up, but they usually make more than one stop and we need to be sure there's enough room for everything on the truck."

"She can tell you. Cassie?"

She appeared beside him. "I heard." She smiled at the woman. "You're a lifesaver."

"That's what we try to do." She handed over a clipboard with a paper and pencil attached.

He knew the implication of her words went so much deeper. Beside him, Cassie concentrated on the form she was filling out.

"How long have you worked here—" he noticed the name on the tag she wore "—Paula?"

"About five years. But technically I'm not working. I have an office job that pays the bills. I'm a volunteer here. It's a way to give back."

"You must find it rewarding."

She nodded. "I do. So does everyone else. It's more than support. We're like a family."

What she didn't say spoke volumes. He could fill in the blanks. "Do all the women from the shelter volunteer?"

She shook her head. "Sometimes just working to put a roof over your head and food on the table for the kids is all you can handle. To keep from going back. The ones who can give their time do it. But not everyone volunteers because they've needed the shelter. It's a good cause and we get people from all circumstances and walks of life who offer their skills.''

"He's an attorney," Cassie interjected. "Divorce," she added pointedly.

"We're always looking for volunteers," Paula said, keen interest sparkling in her eyes.

Cassie touched his arm, and something that looked an awful lot like respect lurked in her gaze. "Can you think of anyone who needs the skills of a good divorce attorney more than a woman searching for a way out of an abusive relationship?"

"You've got a point," he said.

Cassie tapped her lips with the eraser part of the pencil. "I just thought of something. It might be a good way to balance the tally sheet."

"To fill up the well."

"The something more you've been looking for," she added.

Helping women who needed legal aid and couldn't afford to pay for competent counsel. It was a good idea. Hell, it was a great idea. The thought of giving that kind of service brought instant satisfaction.

"I could offer my services pro bono," he said, thinking aloud.

Excitement dancing in her eyes, Cassie looked at Paula. "See? He's brighter than the average bear and not just another pretty face." She rested her hip against the glass counter and folded her arms over her chest as she studied him. "What do you think?"

He pulled out his wallet and found several business cards. He handed them to Paula. "I should have thought of it myself. Everything Old just found its newest volunteer."

Cassie threw her arms around his neck. "You're a good, kind man, Kyle Stratton."

"Don't spread it around," he said against her hair as he folded her closer. "I'm going to need my go-for-the-jugular reputation more than ever."

"It will be our little secret. And when that emotional well of yours runneth over—" She sucked in a breath and squeezed him tight.

"What?" He held her away from him and saw something in her eyes.

"Nothing," she said, shaking her head. "You're one of the good guys. This is merely the place where I get emotional."

Because she had a heart as big as the ocean and soft as marshmallow. Things were suddenly crystal clear. He'd always thought your life flashed before your eyes when you were dying. But he'd never felt more alive as his shell of an existence zipped past his mind's eye. Suddenly he knew what had been missing from his life. What he needed to fill his emotional well. The something more he'd thought there should be in life. He'd known it on some level years ago, when they'd gone on that unforgettable double date with her brother. Now that he'd found her again, he wasn't letting her go.

He only needed to find a way to make Dan understand.

After a picnic supper on the beach, Cassie and Kyle returned to the duplex. She was filled with a sense of contentment that she'd never experienced before. It had been a wonderful day. Kyle had "negotiated" for volunteers from the women's shelter to come by in the morning to pick up the old furniture. Paula was not only grateful for the donation, but the offer of his legal expertise. Kyle had said he thought he was the one who should feel indebted.

The day after the old stuff left, the new stuff would be delivered. That was her cue to leave the beach and start her new job and new life. The thought had made her so unbearably sad she hadn't been able to bear it. Her time with Kyle was almost over.

She had suggested a picnic supper on the beach, fully expecting him to turn her down. Surprisingly, he hadn't. No good deed goes unpunished because all good things come to an end. But why did her punishment have to be so terribly harsh and hurtful?

Cassie unlocked the door to her place and opened it, then glanced back at Kyle. The hanging light fixture in the foyer was lit, casting shadows. In the dimness, she memorized his face, the slight indentation in his chin, his square jaw, the lines fanning out from his puppy-dog eyes, which proved he occasionally laughed. And she knew. She'd fallen in love with him. Again. Soon she would have to say goodbye. Again. And she really didn't want to.

She leaned against the wall beside the door. "Thanks for the pizza and wine."

"Thanks for the beach blanket, the company and the sunset."

"I can't take credit for company and the blanket."

He grinned. "You're too much, Cass."

"It's one of my best qualities."

His smile disappeared as he rested his palm against the wall just above her head and leaned in closer. The amused expression was replaced by a look of such intensity it made her shiver.

"You're cold," he said. "We shouldn't have stayed out so long."

She felt as if she'd been in the cold for years, until this time with Kyle when she'd walked in the warm sun. The discomfort of being chilly was a small price to pay for spending every last second with him.

"Weren't you cold, too?" she asked, trying to shift focus so he wouldn't know he was the source of her shiver.

He shrugged. "It's not macho to admit stuff like that."

"You could have come in sooner. I'd have been fine on my own." From her mouth to God's ear, because she was going to be on her own real soon.

He shook his head. "A gentleman always sees a lady home."

"You're *definitely* a gentleman," she said.

He frowned. "From your tone, I get the feeling you don't mean that in a good way."

"A gentleman also doesn't kiss a lady on a first date. You certainly lived up to that."

"You mean when we doubled with Dan to the high school play-off game."

"Yeah."

"I didn't kiss you that night, did I?"

"No. You were a perfect gentleman."

"I really screwed up that night, didn't I?"

"Yes. You were a perfect gentleman."

"I wanted to kiss you. And this is sort of like a first date."

And last, she thought. But it was probably for the best. Kyle only did no-strings-attached. The one time she'd done strings-attached it had resulted in romantic meltdown. She would be stupid to even think about it again, especially with this man. Unfortunately, he was the only man she would ever want.

"I could kiss you now," he suggested. "To make up for the last time."

"Isn't that sort of like closing the barn door after the cows got loose and partied all night in the pasture? Because we already—you know."

"Yeah," he said. "I definitely know."

The words, combined with the smoldering look in his eyes and the gravel-and-whiskey sexy tone of his voice, made her throb in places she didn't know she had.

His gaze skimmed over her face. "But if you'd rather I didn't—"

Yes, she wanted him to kiss her. All day she'd brushed up against him, playfully touched his arm, but never felt she had the right to take his hand and hold it, have him put his arm around her and nestle her against his side. All the things a couple did. And no, she didn't want him to kiss her. Kissing would lead them to places it would be a mistake to go.

In the end, she couldn't deny herself one last time. "Kiss me," she said.

Slowly he leaned down and captured her mouth with his own. The first wonderful, soft, tender touch drove everything from her mind—right, wrong. Beginning, end. Past, future. There was only now, this moment. She forgot about everything but feeling and remembering.

His lips moved over hers for what could have been hours or minutes. She wasn't sure and she didn't care. Because she was perfectly content with his mouth loving hers, the warmth of his body invading her own. Every moment spent with Kyle made her happy. Kissing him was the icing on the cake. Making love would be even better icing.

Then he traced her bottom lip with his tongue and she opened to him. He dipped inside, taking what she offered without hesitation. With a thoroughness that thrilled her, he stroked and explored the recesses of her mouth. She'd begun to breathe faster and she heard his quick intake of air.

Suddenly he had one arm around her waist, pulling her next to his hard body. His hand tunneled into her hair at the nape of her neck, his palm curving against the back of her head to make the contact of their mouths more secure. She slid her hands up and over his chest, and looped her arms around his neck. Her breasts were pressed to his chest, soft to hard, female to male, and she reveled in the glorious differences between a man and a woman.

The words welled up inside her, clamoring to be heard, but she wouldn't spoil this last time. She would do everything but say she loved him to show him the truth of what she felt.

She pulled her mouth from his and let her eyelids drift open so she could see his face. "My place or yours?"

He glanced at the open doorway beside them. "Yours," he said quickly.

He took her hand and led her through the opening then shut them inside. Looking down at her, he grinned suddenly. And wickedly. "We could play Goldilocks and the three bears."

"As in who's been doing the wild thing in my bed?"

"Yeah."

"I'm not sure I could ever look my parents in the

eye again. And before anything, we need to wash the sand off. I'm afraid I've got sand in places sand was never meant to be.''

''That gives me an idea.''

He took her upstairs and into the bathroom between the two bedrooms. There was a tub, separate shower and vanity with two sinks and a mirror above that took up one wall. The tile floor sported several throw rugs. Kyle reached into the shower and turned on the water.

''This will warm you right up,'' he promised.

''I forgot all about being cold.''

''Good.'' His lips curved upward in a pleased smile. ''But just in case—''

He reached over and pulled her T-shirt from the waistband of her shorts, then slid it up and over her head. Next he unhooked the closure on her pants, tugged the zipper down and she wiggled them off her hips until she stepped out of them. She stood there in bra and panties, wishing she'd splurged on a matching set at the mall lingerie store.

When he reached behind her, she shook her head. ''You have too many clothes on. Let's keep this even.''

He yanked the hem of his shirt up and off. ''Don't have to ask me twice.''

The next thing she knew he'd removed shorts and briefs in one fluid movement and stood naked in front of her. She didn't have to imagine that he wanted her; the evidence of his desire for her was right there. She took him in her hand and his eyes drifted closed as he sucked in a breath. He was a beautiful man, she thought, all taut muscles, flat stomach and long, powerful legs.

With her fingers she explored him, marveling at the soft and hard textures. If anatomy class in nursing school had been this hands-on she would have aced it. She moved up and down over him until he shuddered and curved his fingers around her wrist to stop her.

"Any more and I'll embarrass myself," he warned.

She met his gaze. "Are you ready to wash the sand off your feet?"

"I'll follow you anywhere," he said, his voice hoarse.

She let him go and turned for him to unhook her bra and slide her panties down her legs. When she opened the shower door, semitransparent with steam, clouds of white billowed into the room. She stepped in first with him behind her and the warm water slithered over her head, face and shoulders. Kyle moved in front of her, blocking the spray so it wouldn't hit her in the face.

The stall was spacious, with a shelf for shampoo and other toiletries.

"My feet aren't sandy anymore," she said.

"Let's take care of all those places sand isn't supposed to be. It's the least a gentleman can do."

He reached for the bar of soap and rubbed it between his hands until he'd worked up a luxurious lather. Then he put his palms on her shoulders and worked his way down to her breasts, cupping her as his thumbs brushed her already taut nipples. Electricity shot through her body from the touch, sensitizing every cell, every square inch of skin, every nerve ending.

Before she recovered from the sensory shock, he slid his soapy hand over her slick abdomen and into the triangle of curls between her legs. Slipping one finger inside her, he found the nub at the apex of her femininity and lavished his attention on the single spot.

She gripped his broad shoulders, savoring the sleek muscles beneath her fingers, while she concentrated on standing. As the rhythm of his hand picked up speed so did her breathing. Tension grew within her and she held her breath expectantly. Her chest felt tight, and she struggled to draw in air. The skin on her body tightened until the center of her being shattered. Shock waves consumed her and she braced her forehead against his chest. Kyle folded her in his arms and absorbed her shudders until finally she was still.

She let out a long breath and lifted her head, meeting his heated gaze. "Unbelievable. Amazing. Outstanding," she whispered.

"I'll take that as a compliment."

Water from the showerhead continued to cascade down on them and his dark hair, plastered against his forehead, looked black. She could feel his tension, the way his arms shook as he held her. Her own desire flared to life again. She'd never experienced this intense need before, the yearning to pleasure him.

Slipping her arms around his neck, she pressed her bare breasts against his chest and heard him suck in a breath. He cupped her bottom and pressed her to his hardness.

"I want you," he breathed into her wet hair.

"You've got me."

She clung to him, and he curved his hands around her thighs and raised her, settling her on his hardness. Slowly she took him into her, finally feeling complete. She couldn't imagine anything more wonderful than feeling the man she loved inside her, of being one body—if not one heart.

The muscles in his shoulders and arms bunched as he lifted her again and again, creating the friction to bring him release. Her own yearning intensified. Her breathing grew harsh, just like his. Her heart hammered, just like his. Then her consciousness exploded into golden light as beams of pleasure rippled through her. A moment later, he stilled her and his body tensed as he wrapped his arms around her and groaned out his satisfaction.

He held on to her as her legs slid down and her feet touched solid ground. With one arm still around her, he reached around with the other and shut the water off. Then he opened the door and grabbed a towel from the bar nearby, wrapping her in it before taking the other and securing it around his waist.

After they stepped out of the stall, he cupped her face in his hands, tipping it up until their gazes met. "Cassie, I have to tell you something—"

There was a noise downstairs. "Hey? Anybody here?"

"Ohmigod. That sounds like my brother," she said. She reached over and shut the door leading to the hall. "Quick. We have to get dressed."

"That would help," he said grimly. "But when the you-know-what hits the fan, I'm going to need more than clothes."

Chapter Eight

The both had their shorts on and Cassie was just pulling a shirt over her head when Dan knocked.

"Cassie? You in there?"

"Just a second," she said. Then she whispered, "What are we going to do?"

Kyle knew they had to come out sometime and it was going to get ugly. Dan would have to be an idiot not to realize that his best friend had just made love with his sister in the shower. This was the worst possible way for him to find out about them. So much for breaking the news gently.

"Sis, what are you doing in there? Mom said the painting's not finished. She said you could use help—"

Cassie opened the door. "Hey, big brother."

Dan's gaze skimmed over Cassie, Kyle, their wet hair and her bra still on the floor. In a frenzy to dress, she'd left it there. Her T-shirt clung to her wet skin, leaving very little to the imagination. Kyle didn't have to imagine; he'd just seen every inch of her beautiful, creamy skin moments ago. It was a sight he would always remember.

There wasn't a snowball's chance in hell he would ever see it again. This was a breach of friendship her brother would never forgive.

"Well, this is awkward," Cassie said, standing between him and her brother.

Dan was about his own height but more powerfully built. In his football days, he'd been a defensive lineman to Kyle's quarterback position. His short, light-brown hair was windblown. He must have had the top down on his sports car during the drive up. The jeans and black T-shirt he wore said he hadn't come straight from the office. The icy look in his blue eyes said Kyle was going straight to hell. Yeah, it was going to take more than putting on clothes to smooth this over.

"Give us a minute, Dan," Cassie said, running her fingers through her still-wet hair. "You're going to love this story."

"Yeah?" Dan never looked away from Kyle. "When pigs fly. We need to talk, *buddy*." Then he was gone and his footsteps echoed as he stomped down the stairs.

Cassie stared up at him, her blue eyes huge. "I don't think I've ever seen him look like that."

"I did. Once."

"When the dog was put to sleep?"

Kyle shook his head. "When Stacey Jamison stood him up and he found out she'd eloped."

"Uh-oh. I remember. He wasn't fit to be around

for a long time.'' She stared at the empty doorway for several moments. "But I don't get it. Why is he so ticked off about this?"

"You're his sister."

"And your point would be?" she asked, tilting her head as she looked up at him. "We're unattached, over twenty-one and consenting. What's the problem?"

"You're his *baby* sister."

"Ah," she said, nodding. "So it's a guy thing."

"A definite guy thing."

"Well, I'm going to make it a chick thing," she said, heading for the door.

"Wait." Kyle put a hand on her slender shoulder to stop her. He bent down and retrieved her lacy bra from the floor. "You might want to put this on or it could be more of a chick thing than you bargained for."

"Good point," she said, taking it from him. Her cheeks were pink and he didn't think it was from the shower.

"Give me a couple minutes with your brother, will you, Cass? I think I should talk to him alone."

"Man to man." She nodded, then put a hand on his arm. "Kyle? This guy thing, it's not the sort of guy thing where he would hit you, is it?"

"It would be easier if he did."

Then he grabbed his shirt off the floor and left her, pulling it over his head as he walked down the stairs. Dan was pacing back and forth in the living room, dodging paint cans, drop cloths and furniture.

When he saw Kyle, he stopped and glared as he braced his feet wide apart and rested his hands on his hips. "I thought you were my friend."

"I thought you were mine."

"What the hell does that mean?"

Kyle walked across the room and sat in one of the oak swivel stools in front of the bar, deliberately assuming a nonthreatening position. Cassie had told him friends listen to each other. Friendship was a two-way street. Kyle's only mistake had been thinking he could hang out with her on that street and keep things status quo. Now that his feelings for her were clear, he knew strictly friendship wasn't possible. But maybe Dan would hear him out and understand. Yeah, and maybe he'd flap his arms and fly.

Kyle ran his fingers through his hair. "I expect you to hear me out with an open mind."

Dan let out a bark of laughter, but the angry look in his eyes said he wasn't the slightest bit amused. He stood several feet away and looked as if he were having difficulty controlling his temper.

"If you found your sister Amy and me like I found you and Cassie, would you hear me out with an open mind? Or would you beat the crap out of me first and ask questions later?"

"I like to think I would trust you to do your damnedest not to hurt my sister."

"You never specifically told me to stay away from her."

"That was a long time ago, Dan. I'm not that immature jerk anymore."

"Now you're just a jerk." He let out a long breath and rubbed the back of his neck. "For God's sake, Kyle, Cassie got dumped on not that long ago. How could you stoop so low? Taking advantage of her vulnerability."

"That's not the way it happened. If you'll let me explain—"

"What? Is there a reasonable explanation for stabbing your best friend in the back?"

"I didn't do anything to you. This is between your sister and me. Our choice."

"Not while I'm around." He took a step closer, eyes blazing. "I know how you operate with women. Cassie has always had a crush on you. Everyone knows it. You're here. She's here on the rebound. You make your move—you're the slime of the earth, Stratton."

"Yeah?" Kyle went from irritation to anger in the blink of an eye. "Slime? What is it they say about birds of a feather? Or the pot calling the kettle black? Who do I give a heads-up to about you, *buddy?* Whose brother do I have to warn to watch his sister with you?"

"If all else fails, cloud the issue. Fall back on the tricks of the lawyer trade."

"There's no issue to cloud. If you'd just shut up and listen to me."

Dan crossed his arms over his chest. "Okay. I'm listening."

"Cassie's special. I would never deliberately hurt her. But ever since that double date, when you talked me into going out with her—"

"I saw the way you looked at her. As if she was the cherry on the sundae. I could kick myself for ever setting you up with my sister, thinking I could trust you."

"Why didn't you tell me Cassie had broken her engagement and was moving back from Phoenix?"

A flicker of guilt crossed Dan's face and Kyle knew. "You never trusted me, did you?"

"Obviously with good reason. I told you then and I'll say it again now—you're not the kind of guy I want for Cassie. You're just like your old man. You'll leave her and break her heart."

"What?"

Kyle hadn't noticed Cassie come down the stairs. From the surprised look on Dan's face, he hadn't seen her, either.

"Cassie, I—"

She walked over to her brother. "You told Kyle to stay away from me?"

"Look, Cass, you have to understand. You don't know how guys think."

"Thank goodness. Because from where I'm standing, you think like an idiot. How could you do that to me? To your best friend? Do you have any idea what a mess you've caused?"

"Mess? Me?" he asked. "He slept with you. I was trying to prevent you being hurt. How is this my fault?"

"I'm not talking about now, you—you—" She glared at him, then huffed out a breath. "See what you've done? I'm so darn mad I can't think of a name bad enough to call you."

Kyle knew how deeply Dan loved Cassie, but Kyle had been on the receiving end of the look she was giving him now and it was going to take a lot more than humor to untie the knot in her temper.

She put her hands on her hips. "I'd like to beat some sense into you. But I'm a nurse sworn to help patients get better. It wouldn't look good if I drummed up business. So I'm going to leave until I can look at you without wanting to clobber you.''

She turned on her heel and walked out, slamming the door behind her.

Kyle slid off his bar stool and started to go after her, but Dan grabbed his arm.

''We're not finished.''

Kyle yanked his arm away and looked the other man in the eye. ''We were finished a long time ago. Friends don't judge. They listen, try to help, try to understand. They trust each other. I thought you were my best friend, the one who was always there and never let me down.'' He laughed and the sound was bitter. ''Boy, was I wrong. You stopped being my friend when you didn't trust me enough to do the right thing. Bottom line—friends don't give friends ultimatums.''

A flicker of what might have been regret crossed Dan's face. ''What are your intentions toward my sister?''

''That's none of your damn business.'' Kyle opened the door. ''I'm going to find her and make sure she's okay. Then I plan to talk to her. What I've got to say is between Cassie and me. If she wants you to know, she'll tell you.''

He slammed the inside door then the outside one and jogged down the duplex steps. He remembered telling Cassie he'd lost a lot in his life. He'd also argued a lot of cases in court, and mostly he'd won. But a future without Cassie was staring him in the face. This was the most important argument he'd ever had to make. And no one, not even her brother, was going to keep him from telling her how he felt. If he had to add her to the list of what he'd lost, so be it.

But this time if he went down, he'd do it fighting.

Cassie sat on Kyle's couch and fretted. It seemed she'd been waiting for hours. She hopped up and started to pace. What if he didn't come back? What if Dan had ruined everything? What if—before she could borrow more trouble, the door opened and Kyle walked in.

She rushed to meet him. "Where the heck have you been?"

He put his hands on her arms. "Me? Where were you? I looked everywhere."

"Not quite. I've been here almost the whole time. I figured, after Dan got finished beating you up, you might need a nurse." She inspected him then met his gaze, hoping for a sign he'd been searching for her out of something more than friendship. "You don't look any the worse for wear. So either you took him out with one blow or used words to settle your differences."

"Don't ever do that to me again." He tugged her against him.

"What did I do?"

"You disappeared. I was worried," he said, tightening his arms around her.

She took courage from his pounding heart and tender touch. This might be her last chance to tell Kyle how she felt. If he didn't share her feelings, she would find a way to live with it. But by God she wouldn't have to live with the regret of "if only."

"I have a confession to make." She pulled back enough to see his face. "I wanted to walk my anger and frustration off on the beach. But I didn't. I waited here because I was afraid you'd leave before I could talk to you.''

His body tensed just before he dropped his arms and stepped away from her. ''Obviously you agree with your brother. You think I'm a chip off the old block, the-fruit-doesn't-fall-far-from-the-tree kind of guy.''

''What the heck does that mean?''

''You thought I'd walk out on you.'' There was a look of such stark hopelessness on his face her heart nearly cracked in two.

This was no time to go soft. She had things to say. ''Don't put words in my mouth, Kyle. I don't—''

''Dan's right about one thing.'' He walked away from her into the kitchen, putting the bar between them. ''I'm not good enough for you.''

''My brother doesn't think anyone is good enough. It's one of the things I love most about him. Although while I was waiting here for you, he came over and we had a talk about the fine line between concern and interference.''

Kyle ran his fingers through his hair. ''If he wasn't concerned, he wouldn't have interfered. He was right to be worried about me.''

''Now you listen to me,'' she said. She stood on the other side of the bar and pointed at him. ''You're a good, kind man. A shallow person wouldn't have taken a step back to evaluate his life. A selfish man wouldn't volunteer legal advice to women who can't pay. A less admirable guy wouldn't have backed away from something or someone he wanted just because his friend asked.''

She was hoping he'd wanted her. He folded his arms over his chest. So much for open body language.

"What did you mean before when you said Dan had gotten us in a mess?" he asked.

Here goes, she thought. If he hadn't been attracted to her on their one and only date, if he didn't want her now, she was going to look like the world's biggest fool. So be it. She might as well go for broke.

"What mess? If my brother had kept his big mouth shut and let nature take its course after he fixed us up, we wouldn't have wasted so many years. In Phoenix, I wouldn't have settled for a man who probably sensed I was settling and cheated on me with my friend. *That* mess."

"I had a lot of time to think while I was walking from one end of Carpinteria to the other looking for you."

Her heart swelled with hope. Would he have done that if he didn't care just a little?

"Yes?" she asked, nudging him to go on. "What did you think about?"

"I think when Dan warned me away from you he did me a favor."

"Why?" She could barely get the word out past the lump in her throat. So much for hope. She felt as if he'd stuck a pin in her heart, deflating it like a party balloon.

"I was in a bad place back then. Just a jerk who only wanted one thing. I was confused and sex was easy. But relationships scared the hell out of me. I didn't want to do it wrong over and over like my folks, so I wouldn't do it at all. I was too young and stupid to appreciate you. Eventually I'd have messed up and ruined any chance we might have had. That's assuming I have any chance with you now."

Her gaze snapped up to his. Suddenly hope was

inflating her heart, which began to pound so hard it hurt. "Do you want a chance?" Before he could answer, she asked, "You don't have to be like your folks. Patterns can be broken. I don't believe this is a DNA thing. If two people love each other and commit to staying together, they make it work. Come hell or high water, they'll do whatever it takes."

"Okay. But there's still the issue of kids—" His body tensed and he let out a long breath. "Oh, God."

"What?"

"When we were in the shower, I didn't use a condom." He met her gaze and his was tortured. "I never, ever forget. I'm always careful. Always. It's never happened to me before—losing control like that."

Her heart inflated more, almost to bursting. "I'm going to take that as a compliment."

"This is no time to joke, Cassie."

"It wasn't a joke. I made you forget about protection. Neither of us thought of it."

"What if you're pregnant? It only takes once."

"If it happens we'll deal with it."

"But me with a kid?"

"Don't even try to tell me you wouldn't be a good father." She walked around the bar and stood in front of him. She wanted to get in his face, but height had its limitations. "I saw you with Bayleigh. She adores you."

"But that was a couple of hours, and I'm not responsible for her. She's not mine."

"So you don't like her?"

"Of course I like her. She's terrific. But I've got no training for fatherhood twenty-four seven. Week-ends and holidays with my dad don't seem like enough.''

"You spent summers with my family here at the beach. In between you hung out at my house with my dad. Something had to rub off.'' She threw up her hands and turned away. "Do you think anyone automatically knows how to parent? I don't know how to be a mom, but I want a shot at it. The most important thing is being willing to try. A good parent isn't born or taught. A good parent just shows up through thick and thin, through good and bad—''

"In sickness and health till death do us part?'' His hands curved around her upper arms.

The warmth of his fingers seeped through her T-shirt, heating her everywhere. "What are you saying?''

He turned her to face him. Instead of the dark intensity lurking in his eyes, she saw he was smiling and there was something in his expression she was afraid to name.

"I'm saying you're right.''

She rested her palms against his chest, savoring the strength as she searched his face for a clue about what he was thinking. "What am I right about?''

"Yagottawanna.''

"Excuse me?''

"You have to want to stay together. Marriage isn't easy and you don't walk away the first time there's a bump in the road.''

She blinked up at him. "I'm good, but I'm not that good. How come I got through to you so easily?''

"It's common sense. And readiness. I've heard all this before. I was just never in the right frame of mind for the message to sink in.''

"Oh." She lowered her gaze and focused on the neck of his shirt. "I thought it was me."

"It is you. Someone else could have preached the same sermon to me and it wouldn't have led me to the promised land. But you hit a nerve." He touched his knuckle beneath her chin and nudged upward, urging her to meet his gaze. "Remind me to thank my mother for suggesting I come to the beach house."

"Okay. Why?"

"Because you're here. You are the only woman in the world who could have gotten through to me. From the first summer you followed me around until now, you made me see success in life isn't about luck. It's about showing up. I love you, Cass. I think I always have."

Her heart was full and her eyes teared up. She couldn't believe she wasn't dreaming. He'd actually said the words she'd always longed to hear. "I guess I was wrong about wasted years."

"Why?"

"I think we needed the time and experiences to know this is right. When you've been with the wrong man, it gives you the perfect perspective to recognize the right one. I love you, too. I always have. In fact, I told Dan as much."

"You did?"

"You betcha. He said if you're the guy I want, he'll get behind it, and even though no one is good enough for me, you come pretty darn close."

"He did?"

She nodded. "I know what his friendship means to you. I would never want to cost you that. He said he wouldn't want to cost me happiness. He gave us his blessing."

"He did?"

Cassie carefully watched his face and saw relief sweep into his expression. "Yeah. And he said if you don't ask him to be best man at the wedding, he's going to be really ticked off."

"So in reality we have Dan to thank for getting us together."

"And your mother for sending you here. Matchmaking is in the wind."

"I think that's the sea air, but okay. What does wind have to do with romance?"

"Mandy and Rick got back together because of his mother. Both of them were in the area and she suggested they meet for lunch. She thought they needed closure. In the years following their divorce, neither Mandy or Rick had found anyone else. Instead they found out no other person had worked out because they were still in love with each other."

"And your point is?"

"There's only one right someone for everyone. I know without a doubt that you are my someone."

"And you're mine. I know now it wasn't my career I wanted more from. You're the more I wanted in my life." He bent and lightly touched his lips to hers, then straightened. "I can't ask Dan to be my best man unless there's a wedding. Marry me, Cassie."

One corner of her mouth lifted. "To smooth things over with my brother, or because I might be pregnant?"

"Neither. Because I love you. I want to have children with you. I plan to show up—every day—and be the best husband and father I can. I want us to grow old together."

"I love you, Kyle. There's nothing I want more

than to be with you and have your children. But about old age, I plan to beat it back with a whip and chair and as much cosmetic surgery as I can."

"You will always be beautiful to me." He traced her mouth. "I don't want you for now—I want you forever."

"You sweet-talker." She sighed and rested her cheek on his chest while wrapping her arms around his waist. "You've got me. I would love to marry you. Even though this courtship took you forever."

"Cassie, there's no statute of limitation on courting." He cupped her face in his hands and said, "But for the record, courting is adjourned."

Before she could groan at his play on words, he kissed her. Cassie decided if this was her punishment for good deeds, she needed to sign up for more. Forever.

* * * * *

Don't miss

MIDNIGHT, MOONLIGHT & MIRACLES

by Teresa Southwick.

*Megan Brightwell finds
a one-in-a-million dad
for her very special daughter
in this emotional and heartwarming story
available from Silhouette Special Edition
in January 2003.*